PRAHLAD

Celebrating
30 Years of Publishing
in India

Also by Kevin Missal

Narasimha (Book One of the Narasimha Trilogy)
Hiranyakashyap (Book Two of the Narasimha Trilogy)

BOOK 3

PRAHLAD

THE NARASIMHA TRILOGY

KEVIN MISSAL

HarperCollins *Publishers* India

First published in India by HarperCollins *Publishers* in 2023
4th Floor, Tower A, Building No. 10, DLF Cyber City,
DLF Phase II, Gurugram, Haryana – 122002
www.harpercollins.co.in

2 4 6 8 10 9 7 5 3 1

P-ISBN: 978-93-5489-294-3
E-ISBN: 978-93-5489-503-6

Typeset in 11/14.7 Minion Pro at
Manipal Technologies Ltd, Manipal

Printed and bound at
Thomson Press (India) Ltd

To my patient readers who waited for so long. This book is everything I want it to be when it comes to ending a beautiful series.

AUTHOR'S NOTE

This is to inform you that this is completely a work of fiction. Ideas and themes have been taken from different sources and have been mixed together to produce a comprehensive story and this is by no means the correct order of the events in the original scriptures. Please read this with a motive to be entertained and not educated.

THE TRIBES

DEVAS

The Devas are foreigners who come from the island of Swarg, which lies to the north of Illavarti. They have usurped the northern part of the country and gained control of major cities. Their ruler is called Indra. They worship various elements of nature, like fire, water and ice. They have long lifespans – two to three hundred years. They are really fair and are often associated with the colour white. They are the creators of Somas, which is a blue medicinal liquid derived from the Somalia plants found in Swarg. They believe in Dharma as well as the Trinity Gods – Vishnu, Mahadev and Brahma.

ASURAS

The Asuras are foreigners from the island of Pataal, which is to the east of Illavarti, across the Black Ocean. They are brown-skinned, golden-eyed and worship attributes like strength and valour, rather than the elements like the Devas. They rule the southern lands of Illavarti and their capital is Kashyapuri. They are often associated with evil because they do not have a religion and don't believe in one. They do not partake of the Somas. They have a strong exoskeleton and are competent in battle.

DANAVS

The Danavs are divided into Poulomas and Kalakeyas. The Poulomas are short giants, often ranging from ten to fifteen feet in height, while the Kalakeyas are over twenty feet tall. They live in large towers that are specially constructed for them. They eat large amounts of food and water. They are historically blood brothers of the Asuras and live in Hiranyapur. Other than the need for constant sleep and food, they do not have a purpose in life.

SIMHAS

According to mythology prevalent in Illavarti, the Simhas were created by Lord Vishnu in his first battle against evil. The Simhas are half-lion and half-human in spirit. They wear the skin of a deceased lion. They live in Vaikuntha, the forgotten religious city of Lord Vishnu. Since the Devas are on the side of Dharma, the Simhas fight the battle on the side of the Devas. They are against practices looked at as being related to Adharm. They have strong claws and their skin is pale yellowish. They have reddish beards. This Yug's Avatar is destined to be from the Tribe of the Simhas.

Chronology

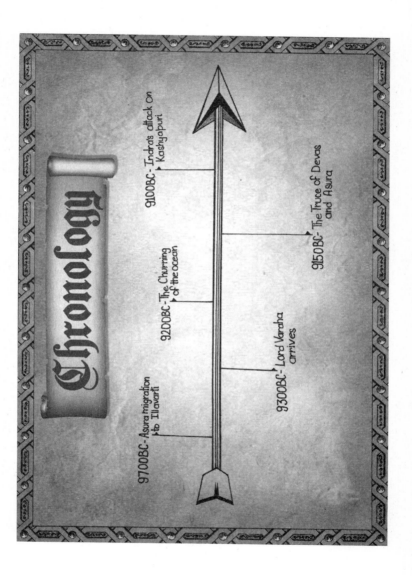

9700BC - Asura migration to Illavarti

9300BC - Lord Varaha arrives

9200BC - The Churning of the ocean

9100BC - Indra's attack on Kashyapuri

9150BC - The Truce of Devas and Asura

THE STORY SO FAR

Fourteen years ago, the truce between the Asuras and the Devas was broken, resulting in the death of the Asura queen.

More than a decade has passed. The instigators of the invasion in Kashyapuri have all but vanished.

As Hiranyakashyap plots his revenge against the Devas, he chooses to follow in his deceased brother's footsteps, leaving the throne to his inexperienced fifteen-year-old son, Prahlad, rather than his firstborn, Anuhrad.

Narasimha, a war veteran amidst the Simhas, is tormented by his past and chooses to lay low with the Manavs. But once his cover is blown, he is urged to join the third Shiva, Bhairav, against Hiranyakashyap's nephew, Andhaka. On the night of the first attack, he successfully vanquishes Andhaka.

Much to his disbelief, Andhaka is reported to have survived Narasimha's attack. As Bhairav ruminates over whether to use the nuclear weapon, Pashupatastra, against their foe, Narasimha wonders if choosing to help these people, after all, will make him the Dharm of this age. It had been prophesied that the Dharm of this age would die prematurely, leaving the fate of this world to the Adharm.

As he goes through his brother's research, Hiranyakashyap finds out that they are descended from Brahma, and are therefore heirs to the invincible armour created from the essence of Avatar Mohini. He seeks to regain the invincible armour by undergoing the Three Trials of Brahma, and then defeat the Devas.

The acting king, Prahlad, investigates an extremist organization, Vishnusena, operating in the shadows of his kingdom. But once he realizes that the leader is Narada, a Manav noble and confidante to his deceased mother, he wonders if the organization is truly *evil*, as labelled by his aunt, Holika. He wonders if the organization's goal of instilling religious faith would bring about reforms in Asura law in the long run.

A horrified Narasimha, having seen the after-effects of Pashupatastra, destroys the weapon and suggests making peace with Andhaka, much to the chagrin of Bhairav. Having won the respect of his Pride and developed feelings for one of the Simhas who nursed him, he believes he is done hiding and might be able to achieve peace without ever becoming the Avatar. As Bhairav expresses his guilt over not having been able to save his own son, they are summoned by Andhaka to negotiate a peace treaty, on the condition that they bring the Pashupatastra.

Both parties meet to make peace: Bhairav's army and the Simhas on one hand, and Andhaka's forces, accompanied by the Asura king's brother, Anuhrad. Andhaka calls their bluff and reveals that he is the long-lost son of Bhairav after all. Bhairav, overcome with emotion, embraces his son, but is stabbed by him as he declares that he is not the same hapless child anymore, but the blind prince, Andhaka. An enraged Narasimha declares war on them and accidentally kills Anuhrad. Anuhrad reveals that he had agreed to support Andhaka's cause, the destruction of the Asura empire, because he felt it would fulfil the desire for vengeance that had overcome him, after his father had killed his true love. But he had realized it only brought him loneliness, even in death. He reveals that there is a reason Andhaka can escape death. He asks a torn Narasimha, who feels he has killed yet another innocent, to protect his younger brother, who remains more virtuous than he would ever have been.

A furious Narasimha follows a fleeing Andhaka and slaughters all of his clones. As he rams the trident of Shiva into the real Andhaka's throat, he, with gritted teeth, embraces the role of the Avatar, come what may. He confides in Chenchen, his lady love, that he was solely responsible for killing innocents back in his prime, and for leading Hiranyakashyap down a vengeful path. And now he has claimed the life of yet another person who was related to him. He states that his only redemption now lies in Prahlad, the current ruler of Kashyapuri.

As Hiranyakashyap just about manages to complete all three trials, he is ambushed by the army of Agni. However, their onslaught bears no effect, as the now-invincible Hiranyakashyap manages to make short work of them all and deliver mortal injuries to the god of fire. With his dying breath, Agni confesses that while his brother, Indra, may have been responsible for the death of his wife, someone else had delivered that fatal attack. That someone was a Simha, bearing the name Narasimha.

Holika confirms her suspicion that Prahlad might after all be allied with the wretched organization that she has vowed to destroy. After losing her adopted daughter in the fire caused by Vishnusena, she confronts Prahlad, whose only hope from the alliance was to bring the Asuras to the light. She kills Narada and calls for the public execution of Prahlad. She tells him that Anuhrad has died in battle, causing anguish to the young ruler. She declares that if his father had got wind of his treachery, he too would have agreed that death was the appropriate punishment for him. As he refuses to let go of his faith in Vishnu, he is chained to rocks and immersed in the water to drown amid the jeers of his fellow men.

Andhaka is later revealed to have survived yet again as he nears Kashyapuri.

In the depths of his watery grave, Prahlad proceeds to relinquish his life only to be pulled out by two familiar hands. The passed-out acting king later wakes up in the company of Dhriti in the village of the rebel force, Vishnusena. As the rebel camp stutters in their future course of action due to a lack of leadership, Prahlad is surprised to know that a suspected enemy has sought an alliance with them—the blind prince of Sonitpur and his cousin, Andhaka.

Meanwhile, Hiranyakashyap, armed with the Brahmshastra, hunts down the few remaining members of the Vishnusena in his kingdom. He is determined to liberate his son from their influence. Joined by his sister, Holika, the arrogant king snuffs out every single life, be it man, woman or child. With Holika looking at him with trepidation, he scoffs at the idea of Lord Vishnu as the protector, while slowly choking a little child to death.

On his way to Kashyapuri, Narasimha encounters Rishi Bhardvaj and his family, who are being attacked by three Pishachas in search of a certain bird-man. Nara makes short work of them, and then discovers that the bird-man was poisoned and is currently under the protection of the rishi. This fugitive is later revealed to be Garuda, chief of the Suparns and the Simha's old comrade. While treating him, Narasimha confides in the rishi that they both used to serve under Indra, especially after the infamous rivalry between the Suparns and Nagas instigated by the Devas. The Devas saw the Suparns as an airborne threat, due to their advanced flying machines, known as vimanas and restricted their supply of Amrit, their primary source of fuel. Their conversation is cut short when an unconscious Garuda bites his hand and transfers the poison to Narasimha. As the Simha physician faints, Garuda is revived.

Sensing that an attack on Kashyapuri is imminent, the Asura king Hiranyakashyap colludes with his sister to launch a pre-emptive strike on Naglok, the abode of Varuna and the reservoir of Deva weaponry and soma. However, with the sudden arrival of Simha mercenaries on the frontlines, he charges ahead without his Brahmshastra, plagued with the fear of Lord Brahma's prophecy–that a Simha will cause his end. Massacring the entire force, he entrusts Holika with finding Prahlad while he himself proceeds with his invasion upon Naglok.

When Narasimha comes to his senses, he enquires about Garuda's situation. The latter reveals it was a result of a failed coup, which resulted in the capture of his mother and the infiltration of the Suparn camp. He also tells him that they have less than a week to find the antidote, the reserves of Amrit, which exist only in Naglok. As they plan to leave for the Suparn kingdom by sea, Narasimha wonders if he is abandoning his oath to protect Prahlad from the Asura king.

Meanwhile, a mysterious figure approaches the Vishnusena encampment, now led by the eldest recruit, Asamanja. Still doubting the new leadership, Prahlad is greeted by Andhaka who brings up the news of Anuhrad's death. Upon being asked about the killer's identity, Andhaka brusquely declares Anuhrad's death as an unfortunate casualty and instead, relays his plans of toppling the Asura kingdom—by abducting the minister of finance, Shand, and plundering the city treasure.

While Chenchen, Narasimha's lover, is treating the wounded, she is suddenly visited by Lord Indra, who reveals that Andhaka has survived and is on the run. Realizing that she could cross paths with Narasimha again, she accompanies the recently widowed Parvati to find the sisterhood of Matrikas, a group of female mercenaries created under Indra's rule. After Chenchen expresses her desire to become a Matrika, Parvati reveals the reason she has undertaken this journey—a prophecy regarding her son, Skanda, which states that he will usher in the great dawn with the help of the seven Matrikas. Meeting the rest, the Manav doctor is tasked with approaching Nrriti, the goddess of death, to find out Skanda's location. She successfully conquers her past demons and passes the test, only to learn that the true Skanda was the son of an Asura and is currently in the company of the

Vishnusena. She later regroups with the Matrikas who resolve to find Skanda.

On the borders of Naglok, both Narasimha and Garuda are apprehended by the Nagas under the command of Jayant, son of Lord Indra. Locked behind bars, they are soon visited by the Deva prince who reveals that Garuda's mother has been dead all along and stomps on her ashes. In retaliation, Garuda chases the fleeing Deva through the streets and throws him to certain death. While travelling to Somgarh to find the antidote, Narasimha refuses to abandon his Dharma and leaves Garuda behind to assist the civilians and Naga guards to oppose the Asura soldiers.

Around the same time, Hiranyakashyap slices through a fleet of ships at Naglok and arrives in the throne room to confront his traitorous cousin, Varuna. As parley, Varuna offers him the captive Narasimha so he can exact his revenge. The Asura king responds by declaring war on Naglok and mortally wounding Varuna. He walks out, only to find Narasimha at the port. Armed with celestial weapons, the two engage in a battle in which the Asura king triumphs over the Simha. He binds Narasimha in chains, vowing to execute him on the same grounds where his wife breathed her last.

Holika, on the other hand, discovers plans for Shand's abduction and sets a trap for their pursuers. As the trio of Dhriti, Prahlad and Asamanja apprehend him, they are chased by Holika until they manage to escape with their target. Even as leaders of the Vishnusena, after interrogating Shand, plot to steal the minting plates from Kashyapuri's treasury, Holika receives a letter from a mole in the Vishnusena informing her about the rebels' plans. As the unaware Vishnusena sneaks into the palace through the sewers, they are caught by Holika's men and Prahlad is taken captive. The mole is revealed to be the blind prince, Andhaka.

When Narasimha is thrown into prison, he wonders whether he can truly become the Avatar. The occupant in the next cell—Prahlad—helps him understand the role of a Vishnu Avatar before being summoned by the Asura king. While Holika begins to doubt her actions and reconsiders her judgment of Prahlad as a result of reading his journals, a perplexed Hiranyakashyap postpones his invasion upon Devlok and instead decides to confront his own son. Despite repeated pleas, Prahlad refuses to change his stance about his father's rule being a stain on the kingdom and demeans him as someone who has succumbed to bitterness and pain. In resignation, Hiranyakashyap sentences him to death via public execution.

However, Narasimha, who has been freed by Andhaka, saves Prahlad from being trampled by elephants and races through the streets of Kashyapuri with the prince in tow, eventually diving headfirst into the river. Out of sight, Prahlad notices the Shrivatsa symbol finally glinting on the Simha's chest, and that is when the latter confides in him that the Avatar of this age would not bring order, but only chaos. He recalls an interaction with Lord Rudra from his past, when it was clearly mentioned that in this age, Dharma would be defeated at the hands of the Adharma, and thus, he must avoid being the Avatar at all costs. As the two slip into the Vishnusena camp unnoticed, they witness the arrival of the Matrikas, and with them, Chenchen, who tearfully embraces

Narasimha. With him still ruminating over the consequences of being the Avatar, Chenchen allays his concerns by telling him that he should rather embrace his destiny. As both parties exchange ideas regarding the capture of Andhaka, they are surprised with a sudden peace treaty from the Asura empire, entreating them to seal the pact in a house of lac.

As the Matrikas and Narasimha plant a decoy to capture the real Andhaka, Asamanja's party reaches the place of agreement only to find a woman wrapped in a strange coat— Holika. Asamanja demands the resignation of the Asura king which Holika declines. He then proposes the revival of idol-worshiping and the reinstatement of Kashyapuri's original epithet, Manavpur, which is denied as well. Asamanja is then ushered out of the house so that aunt and nephew can speak in private. Holika laments the fact that she could have been a better guide to him, and hands him her fireproof coat, explaining that it was all a set-up. Wanting to do right by him, she reveals the weakness of the Brahmshastra. Suddenly, the house is engulfed in flames, and Holika is buried under the rubble. Staggering outside, Prahlad and Dhriti escape. On the other hand, having failed to capture Andhaka again, the defeated Matrikas and Narasimha return to camp. Chenchen tends to Narasimha's wounds and makes him promise that he will not let his anger best him, before sharing a night of passion with him. They resolve to stay together.

In the aftermath of the fire incident, tensions rise amongst the Manav citizens of Kashyapuri who seek death for their king. Hiranyakashyap decides to implicate Narasimha as the culprit and then tend to his people. Since he cannot afford another bloodbath, he launches an attack against the unsuspecting Vishnusena.

Acting on Indra's tip, the Matrikas decide to follow Andhaka to Yakshlok. Just then, the Asura army attacks the rebels only to be thwarted in their attempts by the Suparns led by Garuda. Vowing to end this feud once and for all, Prahlad proposes a pincer attack—he will surrender at the city gates while Narasimha sneaks inside through the sewers. Concurrently, the Matrikas will pursue Andhaka's carriage.

By the time Chenchen reveals that she is carrying Narasimha's child, the Matrikas manage to catch up to the carriage only to find themselves in the company of Indra and his Manav troops. Indra reveals that he had to lure them away for the sake of revenge and that he has already facilitated Andhaka's escape. Since Narasimha killed his son, it is only fitting that Indra claim someone of equal value to Nara. Unwilling to leave no witnesses, Indra attacks the Matrikas. Despite being riddled with arrows, the Matrikas survive; all but one—Chenchen. A tearful Parvati denounces her relationship with Andhaka and proclaims the new mission of the Matrikas—to find and kill him.

As Prahlad is paraded through the streets amid the cheering of the citizens, he challenges his father's claim to the throne and announces that Lord Vishnu is everywhere. A deranged Hiranyakashyap collapses all of the palace pillars, while Narasimha awaits the right time and place to fulfil all conditions for the Brahmshastra's weakness. Seizing the opportunity, he emerges and rips through the innards of the Asura king, bringing an end to the tyrannical Asura bloodline.

A broken Narasimha looks at Chenchen's funeral pyre and decides to embrace his fate as a violent killer than a man of peace. As he enquires after the status of the city which now lies in a power vacuum, he unexpectedly declares to Prahlad that he, Nara, will take the throne of Kashyapuri and bring an end to the oncoming assault of the Devas.

PROLOGUE

A few years ago …

An unbridled sense of hopelessness lingered in the winds of the north.

Whittled down by age and horror, a man stood on the shore, bent over his cane. The snow settling between his toes chilled his bones. The man looked pale, as if slowly but surely inching towards that final moment. Despite the cold, his forehead felt inexplicably warm. He clutched his cane as if it was the last support in his life.

Behind him, his men, two trusted guards with wolves leashed, rubbed their gloved hands together and blew on them, their warm breath fogging in front of them.

In front of the man, the rocky waters of the north gushed and broke against marbled rocks that stood like gods among mortals.

And in all of this, he saw the foreboding.

He waited. He waited for a long time. For an encounter he had never imagined he would be compelled to have. But he did so for reasons he knew best; he had to tell ... *someone.*

He stuck to his word.

At the helm of the first vessel stood the man he was waiting to meet. Almost seven feet in height, he was large, and his golden helmet with its two long horns and his gleaming yellow breastplate made him seem even larger. He had a deadly look about him; his gaze was piercing, brutal and horrifying, to say the least. A fur coat was draped around his immense shoulders and his heavy cloak fluttered in the wind. Long shards of blade were sheathed on his big girdle.

As the boat neared the shore, he jumped off without thinking twice.

It was none other than the king of Kashyapuri.

Hiranyakashyap.

As the fog thickened around them, the two adversaries stood with their eyes locked, sizing each other up. The man with the cane had never thought the day would come when he would be face-to-face with his bitter enemy. He was on the side of Dharma and Hiranyakashyap represented all that was Adharma, but he was acting out of necessity.

'You look exhausted,' Hiranyakashyap said with a smile while his men secured the boat on the shore. 'I'm glad this wasn't some surprise attack.'

'I told you it wouldn't be.'

'Clearly, you are a man of your word. Honest. Unlike me.' Hiranyakashyap grinned. 'So tell me, why have you summoned me this far north? To freeze my bones and balls?'

'And here I thought I would have to wine and dine you before discussing anything.'

'Oh, I'm a man of haste, not patience.'

'All right. Follow me.'

'Is it an ambush?'

'If I said no, would you believe me?'

'Secure the perimeter,' Hiranyakashyap ordered his men. 'If you see anything funny, signal and I shall slit our friend's throat.'

The man with the cane seemed more bored than anything else. He was not impressed by the might of the king, but simply gestured to him to walk along the shore towards the mouth of a cave where water was trickling. Their men did not follow.

'Where have you brought me, old man? What is the sorcery you plan to talk to me about?'

'About our fates, if you'd care to listen.'

'My fate is in my hands.'

They entered the cave, their footsteps echoing in the darkness.

'That is where you are wrong.'

'What do you mean?' Hiranyakashyap demanded, his manner betraying a hint of insecurity.

'How's Kayadhu?' the old man asked, ignoring the question.

'She's doing fine. We just had a child.'

'Indeed.' The old man sighed. 'Give my love to her. She's a good woman.'

'Why are you talking about pointless things? Tell me where we are going.'

They came to a sudden stop. Before them stood a pedestal.

'What is this?' Hiranyakashyap asked.

On the pedestal was a sword that had just the right amount of sheen. Made of intertwined bones and metal, it lay there like a dangerous relic of history.

'Our salvation,' the old man said. 'The one that will save us.'

'This sword ...' Hiranyakashyap came closer to inspect it. 'It's made of ...'

'Bones. Yes. Partly. Mine. My spine.' The old man touched his lower back gingerly, mindful of the pain; the wound was still healing.

The king of Kashyapuri almost gasped in horror. 'Why would you inflict such pain on yourself?'

'Because the prophecy stated that the blood of Shiva must be preserved to kill the Avatar of Vishnu,' the other man said.

'Here we go again.' Hiranyakashyap rolled his eyes. 'Why does it always have to be about this Avatar? There's no such thing!'

'So you say, but I believe otherwise. As you know, the Avatar of Vishnu is supposed to end the world in this Yug and he must be stopped.'

'By whom?'

'By Adharma. You.'

'Your petty bullshit is none of my concern. Your prophecy is false and your charm and Adharma logic don't make sense. I'm as corrupt and as logical as you are.'

'Sure, you must be,' the old man said with a candid, callous expression. 'But we're not here to argue.'

'What do you want me to do with this?' Hiranyakashyap asked.

'Take it with you. Preserve it and use it when necessary.'

Hiranyakashyap picked up the sword and studied it for a while. It had a fine finish to it, but it needed a lot of welding work. It wasn't up to the mark. Even the meekest of his swords would be better than this garbage.

'I can't.' He kept the sword back carefully, out of respect for the other man.

'Why?'

'Because I don't believe in it. If I take it, it would be as good as believing in your nonsense and I would be afraid of this Avatar who would kill me,' Hiranyakashyap said. 'I do not want fear dictating my life.'

'But fear will help you be prepared,' the old man responded.

Hiranyakashyap sighed. He didn't bother to comment on the other man's foolishness. 'A lot of energy went into travelling so far ...' he muttered as he turned to leave. 'I would suggest, Lord Rudra, that you focus on things other than this hocus-pocus.'

And with that, he walked away, leaving Rudra alone and confused. Rudra had never thought he would be rejected like this.

But he believed.

He believed in keeping the sword sacred, away from everything and everyone.

He believed it would be used one day.

CHAPTER ONE

Now ...

Veerbhadra had known about this location for a while.

It was believed to be a myth; people spoke about it in whispers. When he had become Lord Shiva and ascended Lord Bhairav's throne, he had found in his secret compartment papers and maps with mysterious locations that would lead to Rudra's weapon. Sharabha—made from Rudra's spine. His squire had made notes about the weapon when Bhairav was on his deathbed and had kept the information secret for the next Shiva.

But the location ... Bhairav had spent years searching for it, and now Veerbhadra was looking. However, no one knew where it was.

Until recently, when a discovery was made.

An old man in a local town in the north had awoken from a coma. Too old to remember. Too old to be taken seriously. Veerbhadra's soldiers had overheard him saying gibberish ...

about the Sharabha. Apparently, he had been a soldier during Lord Rudra's time and had secretly followed them into the cave—Hiranyakashyap and Rudra.

Veerbhadra hadn't believed the rumours in the beginning, but he assumed Rudra must have had his reasons. He accompanied the old man to the location where the ice-covered gate stood, frozen, looking like any other ice cap out there. A large hill stood at the back, as did a cliff, from where the frozen water would fall if there ever was a sunny day. The shore was lined with wet, snowy plants and the black sea stretched beyond. His men were trying to chisel through the ice while he waited, arms folded, black cape fluttering behind him, cheeks ruddy from the cold and a chill settling deep in his spine.

I hope this isn't a waste of time.

The old man could be wrong. He could be impersonating someone or just making up nonsense.

But Veerbhadra would never give up on a lead. For him, it was simple. He wanted the Sharabha. A weapon so powerful that it would be used *only* when necessary.

Hiranyakashyap was dead now. But evil never dies. It continues to live and this sword needed to be kept with utmost secrecy and safety, till someone found it.

There was a loud crash, followed by cries of alarm from his men. The ice had broken and the frozen glacier had collapsed. His men backed off, yelping in shock. He came forward, unfazed, and saw that blocks of ice were partially blocking the entrance to the dark cave.

'Light your torches,' he ordered his men, and they were quick to comply.

Oiled-up rags wrapped around wooden staves were lit. Veerbhadra led the men inside. The heat from the blazing flames warmed the cold cave. The ice began to melt and water dripped here and there.

'Is this it?' Veerbhadra mumbled to himself.

And then he saw it—a bridge surrounded by absolute darkness that seemed to swallow even the light from the torches. And beyond the bridge was a light that shone brighter than anything he had seen. It was the sword itself, illuminated in the light.

'It's here, men!' Veerbhadra yelled.

His men responded with shouts of triumph and anticipation.

But they should have been careful. For the darkness around the bridge began to move. Veerbhadra realized that this was not water or rocks, but …

People.

Creatures.

Their bodies twisting and contorting, they rose from their supine positions, their shrieks echoing throughout the cavern. Black eyes, black faces, shining golden fangs—Veerbhadra instantly knew what they were.

Bhutas.

Ghosts. Left here by Rudra to act as deterrents to the acquisition of the Sharabha.

Obviously, he wouldn't make it easy.

'Use iron, men!' He scowled and then strode determinedly towards the Sharabha himself, while the soldiers unsheathed their blades with shaking hands and began to fight off the creatures.

Veerbhadra had heard that Shiva could summon the Bhutas to do his bidding, but only those whom he had killed himself. Bhutas were the corpses that had not been given proper cremations. They only did their master's bidding ... the master here being Lord Rudra.

Veerbhadra rushed to the sword and grasped it just as something grabbed his leg. A child Bhuta with burning eyes had him by the ankle. Veerbhadra instantly slashed the sword across the child's face before leaping into the fray. Agile and flexible, the Bhutas had trapped his men and were eating their brains out.

I need to run.

And he did so, but as he made his way through the people, his heart told him not to run. He had to find the sword. Retrieve it. It was the honourable thing to do.

Using his heavy sword, he slashed at a Bhuta who had climbed over one of his men. The Bhuta toppled, and the soldier scrambled to his feet with a sigh of relief.

'RUN!' Veerbhadra commanded.

Immediately, the men fled towards the mouth of the cave. The Bhutas gave chase, screeching and wailing. Veerbhadra rolled over the blocks of ice at the entrance and landed outside the cave, in the bright shining moonlight. Although their cries followed the men outside the cave, the Bhutas remained inside. Bhutas were confined to the location they were summoned to and could only leave if ordered to by their summoner. And that is why Veerbhadra had decided it was better to flee than fight. Those creatures were unfortunate souls who were being used as mercenaries. It would not be right to attack and kill them again.

Veerbhadra looked around. Some of his men had made it out too, but several had got left behind, to be feasted upon by the Bhutas. Veerbhadra took a moment to lament the death of his soldiers, and then he looked at the blade in his hand. It looked like it was made of bones, and the hilt was pure bronze.

'Sharabha,' he whispered to himself. 'The slayer of Dharma.'

CHAPTER TWO

'I saw a monster today.'

Prahlad hadn't meant to say it out loud. He bit his tongue in regret the moment the words slipped out. It was a thought that had raced through his mind—a flicker of hopelessness was the reason for it. He stopped eating and looked across the dining table to where Dhriti was sitting.

They were no longer the street couple they used to be. They were surrounded by gold and glamour. Even their dining table was too long for them to have a proper, intimate conversation. Prahlad looked around the tent he was in. It was one of the many tents set aside for him—the prime minister of Kashyapuri. Even though he was supposed to be running the day-to-day business of the state, he was stuck in the war zone on the outskirts of the city his father had ruled, leading squads in skirmishes and fighting a powerful army.

Indra's army.

The tall banners with the thunderbolt could be seen from afar. Days and nights would go by without knowing who was winning. Prahlad had been a part of a similar war during his father's time, but he had never thought he would be in another.

He had toughened up over the past few months. His muscles had developed, and his face had matured more than it should have. He had scars across his neck and his forehead. And no matter how many times he bathed, his hair remained greasy. He had this world-weariness that weighed him down, making his shoulders slouch.

'What did you say?' Dhriti asked.

The silence stretched between them as Prahlad watched her. She had changed, she was no longer the urchin–assassin she used to be. Now that she was to be wed to him, she had to appear as a proper lady—one who ate well, dressed well and conducted herself elegantly. She was, after all, going to be a wife now.

'I saw a monster,' he repeated.

Her eyes narrowed. 'Where?'

'In the field.'

They could hear the cries and echoes of the battle in the distance. They had been here in the camps for as long as they could remember now.

'Who was it? Indra?'

Prahlad clenched his jaw, recalling the monster. The one in his dreams—and out there.

Prahlad was on the battlefield, but unlike other times in the past when he had been at the heart of it and had fought with all his might, he was on his mare, weighed down by his armour and his helmet, and the heavy girdle at his waist, barking orders. The royal guards stood before him like a shield, challenging the might of Indra's army on the blood-soaked ground that was littered with bodies. Darkness loomed all around even though it was mid-day and the sun shone high in the sky.

Prahlad told his men to march forward and join the battle. 'Strike the left flank!' he instructed, pulling out his sword. Immediately, the archers on his left let loose a volley of flaming arrows that flew in an arc before taking out the enemy soldiers, who toppled on their sides. The other generals and commanders had begun to order their men to join the fray.

'It's under control, Your Highness,' the soldier on the left said to Prahlad.

Prahlad nodded, his gaze fixed on the elephants that were coming now, trumpeting angrily. He watched as they tossed the cavalry and foot soldiers out of the way with their headgear, which had large iron tusks. They were stampeding and destroying and making loud sounds that echoed across the war zone. Prahlad knew well that Indra would send his mutated beasts the moment he thought he was about to lose.

'Use the catapults!' he ordered, distracted momentarily by the sight of someone else entering the battlefield.

Someone he had not expected.

The king of Kashyapuri.

Narasimha.

Bare-chested. His Shrivatsa symbol was glowing eerily under the dark skies. He had no armour, but with his weaponized iron claws he didn't need one. His large lion skin was secured around his shoulders and hung down his back like a cape. The moment he stepped on to the field, everyone began to cower in fear.

Accompanied by the squad that was protecting him, Prahlad urged his horse onward. He watched in horror as Narasimha slashed his way through the enemy soldiers, even those who had given up the fight. There was fear and then there was *fear*. It was the latter that Prahlad saw in the eyes of the enemy. But in Narasimha's eyes there was only anger, and something more—sadism. He could see Narasimha revel in the violence, in his love for gore. He could see Narasimha smiling as he mowed down the soldiers, gutting them. His back was riddled with arrows, yet he continued on his bloody quest.

Suddenly the elephant caught the king's eye. He lurched towards it with superhuman speed, growling, plunged his talons deep inside the animal's body and tore it apart. As the hapless creature collapsed with an agonized cry, its guts spilling out over the people who were closest to it and drenching them with blood, Narasimha leapt on to another animal and dealt it a similar death blow. Narasimha roared again. This time, his roar was powerful and caused chills to run down Prahlad's spine.

'What have you done?' he murmured, still many paces away from the scene that was unfolding in front of his eyes.

Covered in blood, his body a mixture of bronze and scarlet, Narasimha stood with glistening talons, fixing his brutal gaze on the enemy in front of him. Seeing him, the soldiers began to cower and shake. But he didn't let them suffer for long, for he launched yet another attack along with his army, which had rapidly realized that it could fight back and not be smothered by the enemy.

Narasimha didn't flinch as his soldiers went past. His moral duty to uplift spirits completed, he turned his eyes towards Prahlad, who was watching intently with mounting horror.

He was no longer the man he thought he once was.

'How do you tame a monster?' Prahlad asked.

'You are talking about our king,' Dhriti cautioned. 'You do realize what you are saying, right?'

'I don't know any more.'

'You have been having dreams.'

'Yes.'

'Of what?'

'Of destruction and of mayhem.'

'Do you think these dreams are a product of reality? What you are seeing here, you are seeing in your head.'

'Probably.' Prahlad thought about it. 'Probably. I don't know what I want to do.'

'Why don't you talk to him?'

'He's been distant. I try, but he ignores me. But I'll try again. I shouldn't give up.'

'Yes. Otherwise, you know what to do ...'

Prahlad met Dhriti's eyes. She had poison in them.

'Yes. What I did earlier.'

CHAPTER THREE

Narasimha had seen a lot in his dreams, but he had not seen her in a long time.

But he did today, after that riotous moment on the battlefield when he unleashed his anger and forced the world to cower before him. Everyone had feared him and his anger, and he had liked it. He had to just let it go and the symbol on his chest, which he wanted to hide from the world, would glimmer.

In his dream, she was standing on the shore, the wind whipping her hair against her face, her hopeful eyes watching the land. She looked ethereal.

He was without his skin, without his talons—naked.

'Why are you here?'

'To warn you.' She turned to show him an infant in her arms, wrapped up in a blanket.

'Is it … our son?' he asked, teary-eyed.

She smiled. But then her smile turned grim. 'You need to be careful. You cannot let your emotions get the best of you.'

'But they killed you when I was just a healer,' he responded angrily. 'Now that I'm a warrior, they fear me. They respect me.'

'Fear begets fear, not respect. Respect must be earned.'

He gazed at her. 'The enemies we fight—they need to be put down. I know how to do that. I have built my throne, my kingdom, for you. Once I'm done with Indra, I'll be gone forever. I will leave.'

'That's what you think,' she said. 'You will never give up. Don't fall in the same trap as your predecessor. Have you forgotten what happened to him?'

'I killed him.'

'And someone will kill you if you don't stop.'

'Then I shall die a man with a purpose.'

She smiled. It wasn't grim anymore. But it did not reach her eyes either. 'A purpose served in the name of violence is not a purpose.'

Although Narasimha had woken up tired, his wounds were rapidly healing. Ever since the Shrivatsa symbol had appeared on his chest, he had been able to fight on the battlefield for longer. His stamina and endurance had increased, as had his strength. He had received more than he was supposed to.

He emerged from his master tent, set apart from all the others and surrounded by heavily armed soldiers and large gates, spikes and weapons. He was well-guarded.

After all, he was the king.

It had been a long journey to this moment, even though it had taken only a few months. Once he had told Prahlad he wanted to be king, Prahlad had accepted the position of prime minister without protest. Narasimha had met with resistance from the people of Kashyapuri, the majority of whom were Asuras and did not want a Simha king. But they were weak and did not have a king to lead them anymore, while Narasimha had Prahlad. And so, the people had no choice but to listen. Those who protested were allowed to return to their homelands back in the east. On the strength of his alliances with the Suparns and local tribes, Narasimha took over the kingdom, partnering with the Asura ministers who supported him and funded his mad campaign against their common enemy—Indra.

And though during Narasimha's reign their power lessened and the might and rights of the other tribes—Manavs, Yakshas—grew, the Asuras remained quiet ... because of Prahlad. They believed he was the rightful leader, and they knew they were led astray by Hiranyakashyap.

As he meandered through his thoughts, he noticed someone walking towards him. That bronze body and charming smile were unmistakable.

'Quite a spectacle today, lad? Oh jeez, I meant, "Your Highness". He had a twinkle in his eyes.

'Garuda.' Narasimha smiled. 'I didn't see you in the battle.'

His old friend Garuda had joined his campaign, hoping to reclaim the land of his mother that was once ruled by Varuna, but was now run by Indra's satrap.

'I was laying traps along the eastern frontier, where the canyons are. They could attack from there, so archers have been set up.'

'Pretty good.'

'But I heard what you did. Everyone is afraid, I tell you. Afraid!' Garuda chuckled. 'There are a few prisoners of war left from the last skirmish. I believe you should meet. We have interrogated them, but they refuse to cooperate.'

Narasimha nodded. 'Lead the way.'

'You sure? You are still heavily medicated.'

Narasimha rolled his eyes. 'I'm fine.'

Garuda grinned in response, a grin twice as large as Narasimha's, and one that revealed a heart of gold.

Close to the war room, a dozen or so prisoners knelt on the ground, gagged and bound, while the soldiers circled them. As soon as Narasimha arrived with Garuda, the prisoners shrank in fear, their eyes downcast as if before a god.

'They are afraid of you. Ask them what you want. They might tell us about Indra's plan.'

Narasimha didn't respond to Garuda, but walked towards one of the prisoners, grabbed his hair and pulled his head back. Looking him in the eye, he said with a growl, 'You know why I'm here, so speak.'

'He's scared. He knows he can't win.' The prisoner whimpered in response, tears streaming down his face. 'We are but foot soldiers, my lord, please do not kill us. We are paid minimum wages to fight. We do it for our families. I was taken young and trained as a soldier. I do it for my sister. I do it for my mother. I just follow orders.'

Narasimha released the man. He questioned another soldier but did not learn anything useful. He went back to Garuda and told him, 'They are worthless.'

'They can be good slaves. Work as labourers, I believe,' Garuda said.

Unconvinced, Narasimha was contemplating the idea when, all of a sudden, he saw a familiar face exiting the war room. Curly-haired, with thick brows above golden eyes and a lean face, it was the new chief of the Asuras—Vaashkal. He looked completely different from Hiranyakashyap and the other Asuras, who were usually muscled. Narasimha had learnt some time ago that Vaashkal suffered from a degenerating bone disease that hindered his growth. But he made up for his small stature with his flare in politics and shrewdness in business. He had been the minister of coin during Hiranyakashyap's reign, having begun his career at the bottom of the ministry and quickly climbed up the ranks because of his genius. Now, as the chief of Asuras, he was powerful and confident enough to hold his own even in the presence of Narasimha.

'Vaashkal … I believe your place is in the city,' Narasimha said.

'And I believe you should not be torturing our poor prisoners.' Vaashkal smiled. 'But here we are, surprising each other. I came to speak to you, actually. On an urgent matter.' His smile wandered and he looked over at Garuda, who was eavesdropping.

'So speak.'

'Alone is preferable.'

'I am alone.' Narasimha gestured to Garuda to come closer.

Vaashkal sighed. 'And you wonder why I don't tell you my secrets.'

'I tolerate you and your people for your money, Vaashkal. Don't make me reconsider.'

The curly-haired youth came closer. 'This army you have, the grains that feed them, the weapons you use—this is all my money, all right? I own this war, even though you fight it. Without me and my kind, you'd have a pretty hard time establishing coinage of your own and forcing the people to use the new currency.'

Narasimha bit back a retort. Vaashkal was a necessary evil … but only for now. Once he was done with Indra, he would get rid of Vaashkal and the Asuras and set up his own coinage. Till then, he had to listen to their nonsense. 'What do you want?'

'You respond to criticism, so here I am, criticizing. There was an incident of hate violence against an Asura family. Riotous drunkards, Manavs, came in, raped the woman and killed the man. Isn't that a bad sight under your administration?'

'I'm not aware of this.' Narasimha glanced at Garuda, who shrugged.

'How would you be? These things are beneath you apparently, but the city is drunk with your power. They think you will save them; they think you are anti-Asura at heart. The Asura ministers aren't happy and are demanding swift justice from their king.'

'That's Prahlad's job.'

'I know, but I come to you for obvious reasons.' Vaashkal's golden eyes gleamed. 'If you want our support, Your Highness, I believe you should start behaving like a just king.'

Narasimha paused. That seemed like a threat. And he felt powerless at that moment. 'I'll seek an investigation.'

'All right.'

'Garuda shall lead the investigation.'

The Suparn chief was surprised. He was needed here, but he could hardly go against the king.

Vaashkal said, 'I do not care who leads it. But I believe you need to make quick decisions to stay in power. Just like we have given riches, we can take them away too.'

'The riches belong to Prahlad. He's the heir to it all.'

'The court found you guilty of regicide, but we didn't punish you, did we? The people demand justice, give them what they want and they shall be silent.' Vaashkal smiled.

Narasimha felt a burst of anger at being bullied into making a decision. He clenched his jaw and curled his fist. 'All right.'

Vaashkal nodded. 'Thank you, Your Highness. I'm planning to take the slaves with me. We can use them to rebuild some of our broken properties.'

'What slaves?' Narasimha asked and raised his arm.

Immediately, his men let loose a volley of arrows and the prisoners fell to the ground, their cries of shock and pain lingering in the air before fading away. There was absolute silence. Garuda couldn't believe Narasimha had made such a huge decision at such a point.

'That was unnecessary,' Vaashkal said grimly.

'I am the king. I decide what's necessary and what isn't,' Narasimha said and left.

CHAPTER FOUR

Indra had become more than just a title. He had become a person, embodying the name 'Indra'. There had been several Indras before him. Those who had fought for right—and fought for wrong too. The Indras would stand on the side of Dharma.

His real name was Devendra. He was once a young boy who had sought to learn but failed. He had sought to prove himself as mighty, but he had failed. He had seen his parents being killed when he was quite young and he had thought that the world was cruel—and that he ought to bend it to make it better.

Years had passed since then. Now Devendra stood on a hilltop overlooking the battlefield. Nearby, he could see the sapphire tents of his camp, men and women milling about, talking in muted tones around the bonfires. The squads were divided according to their captains. Ravens fluttered across the sky, circling the carcasses of elephants. Indra remained silent, solemnly watching. His eyes were pale blue and his lips were pressed together in a thin line. The thought of his troublesome boy Jayant and the corpse he had found back in Naaglok kept coming to him in flashes. It was a painful memory, a memory he would be unable to forget.

'Are you well?' A voice came from behind.

It was familiar yet distant. It had been so ever since his son's death. He spun around and found Sachi before him. His wife. She was a petite woman, old with soft, curly hair and striking golden eyes. Sachi was a powerhouse in Indra's life, someone who helped and guided him when he needed it. She was the daughter of an Asura, but she had forsaken the Asura way of life and become a Deva when she had fallen in love with Devendra.

'I am conflicted,' he responded. 'We lost another skirmish.'

'Oh.' Her voice was soft. 'But are you well?'

'How can I be?'

'You made an enemy,' she said, putting her hand on his arm. 'You knew the consequences.'

'I didn't know he would end up becoming the bloody king.'

'Well, surprises happen. All you can do now is wait.'

'Wait for what?'

'For his next move.'

'By that time, my army will be gone.'

She paused and then spoke. 'You know why I'm telling you to wait, right?'

Devendra nodded. He didn't want to admit it, but there was another person who was stopping him from going all out. It was his daughter, Jayanti. Young-blooded but wiser than him. She was born late, quite late, but she was incredibly shrewd. She was in Amravati, unhappy with Indra, for she didn't want him to wage this war. She didn't want him to cause more bloodshed. She wanted something else. Far more difficult than what he had done.

Devendra was supposed to celebrate like the rest of his mates, but here he was, in his study, looking at the skies above. He had attacked the Matrikas and chosen to side with Andhaka in the matter, only the latter had now vanished after their deal and he had no idea if he had done the right thing.

There was a knock at the door. When he turned, he realized the guards hadn't detained his furious visitor. She stomped towards him now, her blood boiling, eyes red.

'What did you do?' Jayanti was small in height—after all, she was still a kid. She had her father's eyes and the ferocity of her mother.

'I did what was right by your brother.'

'And he wanted this?'

'He would have wanted vengeance.'

'He was an idiot.' She paused. 'What did you do?'

'I ...' he stopped. 'I was supposed to kill all of them, but I ... I wasn't able to. And one of them, Narasimha's wife ... she died.'

'Narasimha ... the man who is your friend ... the one you talk about ... the one who you are afraid of.'

Indra nodded.

'And you killed his wife?'

There was a secret in her. A secret so deep, only he knew. He had never told her, but she had a hint.

'I see your end, Father. I see your end by your own bloody hands.'

'Do not speak to me like that!' His eyes widened in outrage. 'I did what was right for my blood. You can't let bullies run over you.'

'You didn't even talk to him.'

'Witnesses saw Narasimha throwing Jayant off the Vimana. What else do you want?'

'Not this, at least.' She shook her head. 'I will not support you in your time of need. And you know, *you know* that you need me.' The way she said it, it gave him clarity.

Perhaps she does know. Perhaps she has heard the whispers and gossip.

Only this time, they were true.

'I know.'

She shook her head in dismay and stormed out of the room. Defeated, he stumbled backwards and slumped against the wall, feeling just a tad bit lonely … a tad bit sad.

'You might have to ask her for help,' Sachi said.

Indra shook his head. 'No. I'll figure it out myself.'

A soldier approached them. 'Your Highness, Guru Brihaspati seeks an audience with you. He's in the war room.'

Indra nodded. He kissed his wife and made his way to the war room, where they planned and strategized. He wondered what or who this was all for. It felt as if he was losing not just the battle but everything … everyone. Agni had died. Varuna had died. And the Maruts, his cousins, his brothers, were all perishing. Even though he had lands and wealth, he had no one to share them with.

What is joy if not shared amongst your loved ones? He smiled as Jayanti's voice floated into his mind.

He entered the war room and saw Brihaspati, his guru and the oldest sage of Amravati, waiting for him. He was draped in an ankle-length gown. His wavy greying hair was slicked back with a generous helping of oil. A permanent frown was etched on his round, cherubic face, as if he had a serious problem. Beside him stood Vayu, one of the kings under Indra's dominion. Vayu was the only Marut left; the rest had died. He was the youngest of them all and quite handsome, with a sharp nose and beautiful grey eyes.

And he had a power. He could control the winds.

'To what do I owe the pleasure?'

'We are losing,' Vayu growled. 'My armies are dying here, Lord Indra. We need to have a contingency plan. Ever since the bloody mongrel has sided with Asuras, he's been having a pretty smooth ride.'

'And what do you think I should do?' Indra asked. 'I have sent my elephants. I have sent my finest men. We are dealing not with a man, but with a god.'

'And only a god can stop him,' Brihaspati said. Only he knew the secret. 'I believe it is time to end it. Bring forth the Vajra.'

'And destroy all of Kashyapuri?' Indra scoffed. 'I've caused enough destruction for one lifetime.'

'It is for Dharma, of course.'

'But isn't Dharma peace?' Indra asked. 'Are we not all propagators of peace?'

Both of them were silent. Indra walked to the long mahogany table and took one of the apples kept on it.

'I cannot release a nuclear weapon,' he said, biting into the juicy fruit.

'Why?' Vayu asked.

'I made a pledge to someone.'

'So we will lose,' Brihaspati said. 'A promise can be broken if it is for the greater good.'

'We have to find another way.' Indra shook his head. 'My daughter ...'

'Don't bring my niece into this.' Vayu shrugged. 'She's a child. We are generals of bloodshed. Sage Kashyap wanted us to have these powers to rule this country in the most dharmic way. When people fight against Dharma, we fight back, or have you forgotten that? That was our objective. That is why we fight ... or at least I do. You lost it somewhere.'

Indra nodded, dismayed. He had lost his powers a long time ago. But it had been for the greater good. Now he was just an old man with regrets. 'I have been thinking about something.'

'And what is that? Teaming up with Andhaka again?' Vayu chuckled.

'He's vanished, so no.' Indra shook his head. 'It's something I should have done years ago.'

'What?' Brihaspati spat.

'A truce,' Indra said, 'a truce with Narasimha.'

CHAPTER FIVE

Parvati was running.

She was running towards something, but she didn't know what. She was barefoot on the snow, partially naked, but she had made sure that her son was wrapped well in the blanket. She could bear the horrors of the environment, but she couldn't let her son do so.

She was young. Her dark hair streamed behind her as she ran from the mayhem and the violence that was being perpetrated.

A loud explosion made her son start crying. She stopped, breathless, and comforted him. 'It's all right, my child, it's all right.'

But it wasn't all right at all. A cloud of smoke billowed in the distance. She was surrounded by snowy hills. Her eyes were drawn to the misty skies where the sun was hiding despicably.

I have to find Bhairav. I need to find him …

He had vanished somewhere. She couldn't remember how or when.

As she kept moving, she could see that the smoke was rising from behind the fort in the north. Her fort. Her home. Which had been attacked by King Hiranyaksha's bloody mongrels. Hiranyaksha, the king of Kashyapuri, and brother of Hiranyakashyap.

Parvati trudged further till her feet began to give up. She looked around for some shelter, a hut, a cottage or a village … but there was none. Despite the weariness and fatigue, she pushed herself to keep going.

All of a sudden, she heard the familiar sound of hoofbeats. Horsemen!

They were coming up the path, towards her. Relief washed over her. She could ask for a ride to a nearby village where she would lie low until she figured out what to do next. As the horsemen drew closer, she noticed they were larger and taller than average. They were wearing black armour and dark helmets and their eyes were … bronze.

A chill went down her spine.

Asuras.

'Look who we have here! If it isn't Shiva's woman!' One of them chuckled. 'Should we just take her or bury her here?' he asked the others. The rest were quiet. Slowly, they began to circle her.

Weak with cold and hunger, Parvati shrank in fear.

'Let's just sever her head and be done with her.'

'Or just leave her be? She has nowhere to go. The cold will take care of her,' another suggested and there was a loud cackle.

'Perhaps.' The first Asura dismounted and sauntered towards her. She tried to run away, but he grabbed her by the shawl and flung her to the ground.

Dazed from the pain, she realized that the Asuras had her son. She made a desperate attempt to snatch him from the Asuras towering over her, but he pulled him away, laughing.

She began to cry and whimper. She wished she could fight them, revive the Matrika in her, but she was terribly weak. She had given birth just a few days ago and was about to pass out. But she still tried ...

Suddenly, they heard the sound of trumpets blaring and hooves thumping against the ground in the distance. Momentarily distracted, Parvati and the Asuras turned to see ...

Bhairav, with dozens of his men, was racing towards them.

The Asuras started to flee. One of them wanted to grab hold of her too, but another said, 'Leave her!'

As the Asuras galloped away, Parvati saw that they were taking her child. She grabbed hold of one of the Asuras and tried to stop him, but he stomped on her arm and kicked her aside. She yelped in pain and drew back.

The Asura leapt on to his horse and raced after his mates.

Parvati was left all alone. Her black hair was now crystal white, covered in snowflakes.

She opened her eyes.

She was lying on the ground, under the starry sky. Alone. She looked sideways after hearing a sharp shrill sound and saw who it was.

The Matrikas. Sitting around the bonfire, just like the time when she had brought Chenchen.

Chenchen …

Oh, the poor woman. It was Parvati who had lured her. Brought her to Nrriti. Made her part of the Matrikas. Among whom she had found her liberation, but also her damnation in the end.

Bloody Andhaka!

She had called him by his birth name once, but now, for her, it was non-existent. He wasn't the person she had had to forsake years ago. He was a vicious monster. Hiranyaksha had made him horrible. Filthy. Evil.

But Bhairav had always said no one was only evil … everyone was the hero of their story.

Andhaka would reach the end in his own twisted way. He had not known she was pregnant …

Why am I justifying his actions? Motherly instincts! I have to kill them.

Parvati dismissed her thoughts and made for the bonfire, where she saw Chamundi, Narsimhi, Brahmani and the other Matrikas. They were all discussing their next move.

They had left Narasimha and Prahlad after the attack. Parvati had wanted to stay, but Brahmani had said that their war was not with Indra but with Andhaka. He had to be taken down—no one else. He had hurt her. Indra was just a weapon used by Andhaka.

He was the root cause of most of the evil around them, and to kill the root cause would result in the defeat of Indra himself.

They were outside the village, in the north-east where the winds were turbulent. They had been following his trail. Asking around, learning more about him in the process, bit by bit. He was travelling with his band of men. He was not easily distinguishable. For those who saw him actually saw him. And they noticed his footprints were headed north-east.

Why though? Why was he running away from everything? He was someone who enjoyed being at the heart of conflict and yet here he was, somewhere obscure.

'What have we decided?' Parvati asked. Her eyes were puffy.

Brahmani said, 'We are waiting for a contact. He said they saw him in the village few days back, but they're not sure where he went.'

Parvati nodded. They had been paying gold or silver, or any coin they could get their hands on, in exchange for information, even doing odd jobs to help someone in need in return.

'Are you okay?' Brahmani asked.

'No. But do I have a choice not to be?'

'You don't have to be there when we do it.'

Parvati clenched her jaw. 'I know. I just want to help you all.' She didn't know whether she would even be able to face Andhaka. Gaze upon his lifeless body. All her life she had thought her son was dead, but he was alive. Very much so. And wreaking havoc.

'We know,' one of the Matrikas said.

Parvati didn't know all of them because she had been feeling very distant from everyone. She was feeling frustrated and anxious at the same time. They decided to wait for a while, and Parvati went back to sleep. She knew Brahmani would be able to handle matters. However, as she began to fall asleep, she saw something move in the shadows ...

Then another thing ...

She could feel something was wrong. It was perhaps instinctive, but she turned around to look at her group. They were oblivious—still discussing. Even the panther that belonged to Chamundi was snoring lightly.

I should warn them ... or am I overthinking this?

But before she could say or do anything, an arrow whizzed through the air and embedded itself in her shoulder. She fell back on the ground with a thud. The sound alerted the other Matrikas, who instantly drew their weapons to attack the unknown enemy.

But the enemy didn't remain unknown for long. A rusty-looking bandit emerged from the forest and walked up to them with a scroll in his hand. More people with crossbows and bows and arrows followed, ready to attack the Matrikas.

Parvati was in excruciating pain. She tried to pull out the arrow, which was hurting her terribly.

'A message from your friend. "Do not chase me. Do not follow. Where I go is where you will fall. Stay away."' The bandit stopped reading the scroll and threw it away. 'I believe your friend doesn't like you. Nor do we, since he paid us to not like you.'

Parvati crawled to her bed, where she had kept her dagger. The arrow still in her shoulder, she grabbed the dagger and let it fly with a pained grunt. The next instant, the bandit was on the ground, a blade sticking out of his thick skull.

At the sight of their fallen leader, the other bandits were thrown into confusion. The Matrikas seized the opportunity and challenged them. A trident was thrown towards another bandit, while a noose grabbed one by the throat and pulled him, choking him and twisting his neck. A few of the Matrikas helped Parvati get away from the mayhem, just as she had done years ago. She was once again powerless, broken, and she couldn't take it any more. She wanted to be free from the hurt and the pain.

I can't go back. I can't run again. Last time I did—I was alone.

With the little strength that she had in her, she pulled out the arrow. Blood gushed from the wound, but she tore a strip of her dhoti and wrapped it across her gash with some help. A sudden shriek caught her attention. When she looked in the direction of the sound, she saw Brahmani on the ground and a bandit pointing a spear at her throat. Parvati sprinted across and hurled herself at the bandit, who was taken by surprise. He stumbled backwards, losing his grip on the spear. Parvati grabbed the fallen spear and stabbed the bandit. When she turned around, the Matrikas had defeated and killed most of the other bandits. She held out her hand to Brahmani and helped her up.

'Thank you. He knows we are following him.'

'He has ravens around. Of course he does.' Parvati smiled. 'But there's one bit of good news in all of this.'

'And what would that be?'

'We are on the right path,' Parvati said.

CHAPTER SIX

Kashyapuri wasn't what it used to be.

The city looked ravaged, like the earth after a battle, or a raven after a hunter's meal. The smell of rot permeated the streets and alleys. There were sounds of welding blades, and cries and sobs rent the air. There was no peace, no tranquillity. Only horror all around.

It was as if a plague had caught hold of the city.

Garuda wondered if his friend Narasimha had played a part in it.

Probably. He was the king, yet he wasn't. He had appointed deputies to run the state while he went about exacting his revenge, but running a city was about more than just appointing people. It was about being present.

Garuda, along with a few of his Suparn guards, was making his way through the city. Beside him, with his own set of men, was Vaashkal. Garuda turned his head and looked at him. There was something sinister about the Asura. Perhaps

31

it was his nose or his shrewd golden eyes. Perhaps it was how beautiful he was. Or perhaps it was the fact that he resembled someone Garuda had met …

Who …? Garuda couldn't quite put a finger on it.

But whatever it was, it was bloody irksome.

'How far are we from the slaughter?'

'Oh, just around the corner. Enjoy the scenery until then.'

Garuda shook his head in disgust. His nostrils flared at the scent of the decrepitude all around. Rats scurried. The sewers were smelling. The people lining the streets looked at them with venom in their eyes. Some even shouted and threatened, only to be pushed back by the guards. Garuda was not surprised that Narasimha didn't want to come here. It was a living reminder of the actions he had committed. By performing regicide, he had invited the people's wrath. The only thing that was working in his favour was Vaashkal and the team of other ministers.

'We're here.' Vaashkal's voice broke into his thoughts.

The house was surrounded by people, their anger palpable. The guards shoved their way through the crowd to clear a path for Garuda.

Garuda had been a kind man all his life. He had loved his mother. And though he had been wronged, he had never hated the world for that. He always saw silver linings in the most dire of situations.

But here …

He saw hatred. He saw horror.

Lying in front of him were two people. A woman, burnt and scalped and a man whose limbs had been twisted, broken and destroyed.

As the bile rose to his throat, he ordered his second-in-command, 'Get rid of the people who have gathered here.'

The guards pushed the people away, and that led to more of a problem. The crowd began to spit and retaliate.

'We need our city back!'

Someone threw a stone at Garuda, which he deflected with his gauntlet.

'Get them out of here!' Garuda shouted.

'You are a monster!'

'Your ruler is a monster!'

'We are ruled by evil!'

The people protested as they were dragged away.

Garuda stood silent, alert. Once the crowd had cleared and his guards had surrounded the crime scene, he knelt down and examined the corpses. He turned and saw Vaashkal observing him.

'I believe you are not liked by the public much,' the Asura remarked.

Garuda ignored him. 'All this is the result of a drunken brawl?'

'Indeed.'

'Doesn't look like it.'

The local soldier who had first identified the bodies had been standing to the side, shaking like a dry leaf in the wind. Garuda gestured to him. 'Where did you find it?'

'It was right outside the tavern, my lord.'

'Any witnesses?'

'Happened in the dead of night, my lord.'

'The taverns close early, do they not? So it happened after that.'

'By the looks of it, my lord, they are a couple. They must have been …'

Garuda nodded. 'Yes, I believe so. Do we have any suspects?'

'Yes, they were caught red-handed, literally. They confessed and were crying.'

Crying? Interesting.

Garuda got to his feet.

Vaashkal said, 'I believe you should meet them. They have lovely blue eyes, Commander Garuda.'

Garuda nodded, catching on to Vaashkal's cryptic remark—the culprits were Nagas. 'Let's go!'

The prison had a long corridor with a wall on one side and cells on the other. The inmates yelled and scowled at Garuda as he passed by. After the war with Narasimha and the regicide, a lot of those who were against Narasimha were imprisoned as a way to silence them.

Vaashkal stopped outside one of the cells. Garuda peered in through the bars and saw two people cowering in the corner. The soldiers unlocked the door and he entered, followed by Vaashkal. Garuda looked at the Nagas. The very ones that Narasimha supported. As a Suparn, he had never had any fascination with them. But right now, he pitied them.

'Why did you murder the two people?' he asked straightaway.

They shivered. They were afraid. They couldn't speak.

'Say it,' Garuda demanded sternly. 'Say it, damn you!'

'We—we—we were paid to do so. We—we—we did it for money. That's all. We are beggars. Scavengers.'

Garuda nodded. 'Interesting. Who paid you two?'

'We don't know. It was a soldier … no … a … a merchant—' They broke off, sobbing. 'We don't know who it was.'

Garuda nodded. 'But you killed and for that there's no forgiveness. You shall pay for it.'

With that, he ordered the prison superintendent to prepare for the hanging. As he spoke, he noticed Vaashkal smiling.

That little rot has a hand in this for sure. Otherwise he wouldn't be so gleeful about it.

'Find the person who paid them,' Garuda added. 'I am certain he's somewhere around here—like a rat eating us from the inside.'

Vaashkal's smile faded abruptly.

I have my eyes on you, Garuda thought.

CHAPTER SEVEN

Love fades.

Not the way you would think. It fades into oblivion. It fades in absolute corruption.

Narasimha could feel his body tremble as the horrors of his dream grasped at his bones and skin and tore them apart. He was convulsing and sobbing, drenched in tears and sweat. But the thoughts weren't stopping. He could see in the darkness …

Love.

It flickered like a star. Burning with hot embers, but dying as quick as the snow melts.

Chenchen.

Horrible, discerning.

She was bright in the darkness. She was smiling. But she had tears in her eyes.

'What are you doing?' she asked.

'What do you mean?'

'You shouldn't do what you are doing.'

'You are not real. You died,' Narasimha blurted out, tears in his eyes.

'The fact that you said it—that is what makes it real.'

He paused. She was *not* dead. At least not in his heart. And yet he had just said it. He felt a pang of guilt, even though he knew she was not real, just an illusion created by the wonders of his mind.

'I am not doing anything wrong.'

'You don't realize it now. But when the sun sets, and you are in the midst of fields with a silver blade on top of you—that day you will be a man dying with regrets.'

Her words sounded liked an omen.

'I am doing this for you.'

'Isn't that what Hiranyakashyap said? The throne is making you the person you killed,' Chenchen said, walking close to him. She didn't have the child now, unlike the last dream. 'You don't belong here, my love.' She touched his face, her fingers gently caressing his eyelids and his nose.

He didn't have his mane. He felt vulnerable and naked without it—just the way he liked it with Chenchen.

'I belong with you,' he said softly.

She nodded. Their heads met each other. And they both wept.

'Be careful of the whispers,' she said, cupping his face in her palms. 'There's venom around you.'

Narasimha woke up with a jolt.

He couldn't breathe. He felt as if a weight was pressing down on his chest, making it impossible to draw in his next breath. He drank the Madeira next to his bed and tried to compose himself. The morning sun had staked its claim across the tropical sky.

Need to start the day.

He made his way to the war room, his guards following him. He had tied a golden dhoti around his waist, and the Shrivatsa symbol on his chest was glimmering. His eyes were dark and hollow. He sighed deeply as he entered the room only to find someone already there, playing with the figures on the map table.

The curly-haired horror …

Narasimha didn't like Vaashkal. Couldn't stand him, actually. Especially since Garuda had mentioned what Vaashkal was up to. He had a hand in the Asura murders—for reasons Narasimha didn't know yet. Narasimha was a warrior, a soldier. He could go out and annihilate his enemies on the battlefield with ease. Here, in the war tents, surrounded by his army as well as the ministers, he had to play politics to survive. But he didn't know how to do that or whom to believe; he was helpless.

Narasimha merely nodded to Vaashkal and made his way to the wine table, where he poured himself a glass. He didn't allude to what Garuda had told him; he didn't want to alert the enemy.

'You know, Your Highness, what you drink is what I create. I have a winery and a great garden where I grow the finest grapes. You should visit it sometime. I have a fascination with growing things out of nothing,' Vaashkal said. 'When I was a child, an adopted one at that, my father was a gardener at a local lord's house. And what a charming man he was. Taught me all kinds of things about manure, soil and plants. You know, I love one plant in particular—the nightshade. What a beautiful name it is, isn't it?'

Narasimha had seen plenty of enemies. They tended to be husky, large and scary-looking. But not this fellow. He was short, handsome and charming, with a disarming smile.

Is he really an enemy?

'Then I should thank you,' Narasimha said. 'The Madeira has been keeping me busy.' He smiled to himself as he emptied the goblet in a single swallow. 'What are you doing here?' he added shortly.

'I thought you'd be in a better mood in the morning, but that doesn't seem to be the case.' Vaashkal rested his arm across the back of chair. 'Indra sent a raven. Care to listen to it?'

'We should have torn through the raven's chest before it reached us.' Narasimha's eyes narrowed.

'Ah, but then we might have missed the message.' Vaashkal paused. 'Indra has declared truce. Cause for celebration?'

'Truce?' Narasimha growled.

'Oh yes, he's ready to surrender all the lands except Amravati. And give us fifteen per cent of the gross revenue that he earns as taxes from his capital. Now that, I believe, is a deal one can't pass up.'

Narasimha remained stoic, swirling the wine in his goblet, listening quietly. 'And in return, he wants to retreat?'

'Yes, mind his own business.'

'You have talked to the council?'

'I thought I'd bring this offer to you first ... unless you have something else in mind.'

Narasimha was quiet. There was a lot of anger in him. He felt belittled.

'Did he think this was about some money? This was about far more than that!' His eyes narrowed in anger and he threw the goblet aside with brute force. There was a thunderous clatter and, for a moment, there was a flicker of fear in Vaashkal's eyes, but he composed himself.

'You need to look beyond your anger, Your Highness,' Vaashkal said. 'You need to think about the kingdom you are ruling over.'

I don't care, Narasimha almost muttered.

He cleared the table in one mighty swipe, toppling the wine carafes and spilling their contents on the ground. The goblets met the same fate as their mate, clattering helplessly to the floor. Narasimha grabbed hold of the table and broke it in two with a loud crack.

The violent sounds brought the guards running inside, but they stood quietly in a corner.

'I have an idea,' Vaashkal drawled unconcernedly, ignoring the havoc Narasimha was wreaking. 'There is a story. And I shall tell it to you if—'

Narasimha lunged towards him. 'I do not want to hear your puny stories!'

'Oh, but you need to hear this one. It pertains to you,' Vaashkal said with a smile.

Narasimha clenched his jaw and fist and stepped back while Vaashkal stood up from his chair and poured some wine from a dented carafe into a broken goblet. 'There's a certain sense of poeticism associated with broken things.'

'Get on with your story. My patience wanes.'

'Once a king, a god actually, decided he had too much power. He was tired of it. He knew it was destroying him from within. But he continued to use it. Controlled the world, so to speak. But things began to change when his daughter was born. Though he had lived a horrible life, he was ready to do anything for his daughter and help her live a righteous life, not like his.

'But something was wrong. Perhaps his karma. He had done horrible things when he was young and karma got back at him. He was forced to see his infant face troubles breathing. No amount of Ayurveda could help her. He was worried. He went to shamans and magicians and sorceresses, but no one could cure her. Until …'

Vaashkal smiled. 'Nrriti, the goddess of death, told him what to do. "Give the power to your daughter," the goddess said. "A part of you will be in her and, in return, I will grant her life."'

Narasimha's anger began to fade as he listened intently. He knew where the story was heading and who Vaashkal was talking about.

'And so he did. He lost all his power, but he got her in return.'

'I know who you are talking about.'

'Everyone does now that it has become a myth. Isn't this how myths are created?'

Narasimha growled under his breath. 'What are you trying to imply?'

'What I'm trying to say is—either find truce with him and rule the kingdom in peace or, if you are so desperate for revenge, then play the part right.' He paused. 'You hurt him where he hurt you.'

'You are mad!' Narasimha was shocked to realize what Vaashkal meant.

'Am I? Was he?' Vaashkal asked. 'I have looked at the problem from every angle. This is the best solution. You'll be able to get the power that he has kept within her.'

Narasimha strode forward, wrapped his hand around the Asura's neck and lifted him off the floor. Vaashkal whimpered in horror and pain. He was on the brink of tearing up or fainting or both, for he couldn't breathe and his eyes were beginning to bulge.

'Do not tell me these horrible ideas,' Narasimha growled, his anger spiking. 'I do not know what you are up to and why, but I know one thing. If I figure out your ulterior motive, it'll be bad for you … very bad. I fear for you.'

'You are … wrong … w-wrong …' Vaashkal coughed. 'I only want to do right by you. I want to help you.' He gasped. 'You will understand later.'

'Then why do you suggest such horrible ideas? Actions that'll make me look more like a tyrant than a man on a mission for love.'

Vaashkal struggled to speak. 'I tell you because'—he coughed—'you might need that power to defeat your enemies …'

'What enemies? I don't have any,' Narasimha said, shaking Vaashkal in frustration. His Shrivatsa was glowing brightly, almost blinding the Asura.

'There might be some stir among the Danavs …'

Narasimha released him as soon he uttered this. Vaashkal lay on the ground, wheezing, trying to catch his breath amid bouts of coughing.

'What stir?'

'The Danavs might not be leaving. They might stage a coup. I have been trying to control them, but they could be a problem.' Vaashkal cleared his throat. 'Worst-case scenario, you might require some energies of a god to defeat them.'

'I'm already a god.'

'That's what a god would never say.' Vaashkal coughed again and leaned against the wooden poles holding up the tent. 'I don't think the Danavs will be a problem, but it's better to be safe than sorry.'

Narasimha exited the tent, ignoring the guards who came to attention when they saw him. Vaashkal's words echoed in his mind and he found himself wondering. *Is there another way? There has to be.*

Otherwise, it would be a problem.

A big problem.

CHAPTER EIGHT

Prahlad clearly remembered the day when it had happened.

It was night. The sun had disappeared beyond the horizon and, once the storms had taken their toll, a few stars had hesitantly emerged in the dark sky. Prahlad was in his balcony, waiting for the moment when he would meet their dear god and saviour, Lord Narasimha. Things had been in disarray ever since his father, King Hiranyakashyap, had died; the city of Kashyapuri was in turmoil. There were debates and discussions in every corner of every lane and endless quarrels. Every idea, every proposal, every suggestion was met with fierce opposition, and the odd assassination attempt. Still, he made a vow to stand by Narasimha through all of it.

Narasimha fought back too. He fought through rigidity. He fought through problems. Prahlad supported him like a dutiful brother, a son and a friend.

'How do you see the world in front of you?' asked a voice.

He had been waiting for the man, hoping to have a conversation that he had not been able to have for a while now with him. They used to talk once, but now everything had gone to oblivion ...

Tonight felt different though.

'Oh, you finally got done,' he said with a smile.

Narasimha nodded. 'Have you had dinner?'

'A duck, perhaps. And you?'

'Asparagus.' He growled. 'My stomach is troubled. It requires meat, but I have abstained.'

His eyes were tired. He wore his mane and his face was shadowed, but there was no mistaking the hurt and hollowness in his eyes. Prahlad had avoided talking about Chenchen. It would hurt Narasimha grievously and he didn't have the heart to put the other man through that again. He still remembered the day they had found out ... Narasimha had cried for hours and his growls had been louder than the ravens of the night. And when he proposed to be the king ... Prahlad knew something was wrong.

But not now. The man in front of him was tired and hurt, but not evil. Not the kind he saw at the antyeshti, the funerary rites.

'How is it going, the transition?'

'Pretty tough,' Narasimha said. 'Though I did manage to take out time to do something for you.'

Prahlad narrowed his eyes and arched his brows. 'And what would that be?'

'I got a jeweller to fashion something for you. It's cheeky, but there's no better way to thank you, so be grateful.' Nara came forward, awkwardly, with a rough smile, and handed him something.

'What is it?' Prahlad murmured and then glanced at his palm.

It was a ring. The central stone resembled a mix of topaz and sapphire. Something was etched on top of it—a symbol that was very much akin to the one that Narasimha had on his chest.

'The Shrivatsa symbol.' Prahlad smiled.

'Yes. I remember you believe in it, in Lord Vishnu's Avatar.' Nara smiled back. 'I might be one and I might not be, I do not know.' He paused. 'But this holds more value than that. It holds the value of hope. That everything will be all right. If not for me, then at least for you.'

'You need it more than I do.' Prahlad chuckled. He was teary-eyed as he slipped on the ring. No one had ever gifted him anything, not even his father, and now here was Nara with this precious gift … making him grin like a fool.

'I have one too.' Narasimha showed him the ring on his finger, which Prahlad had failed to notice until then. 'The same as yours. As a remembrance that no matter how dark the days are, we shall be beacons of light.'

Prahlad smiled. He had been praying to Lord Vishnu to bring sanity to Nara. Perhaps his prayer had been answered. Nara seemed human again. And Prahlad wanted to hug him, but he felt a tug of embarrassment and nodded instead. 'Thank you for this.'

He looked at the ring again …

The ring was dirtier than ever. And no amount of soap would be able to clean it.

He was at the dinner table, looking at it, remembering the conversation he had had months ago—one of the last heart-to-hearts he had had with Narasimha. Things had spiralled out of control after that. Now their conversation was just a memory. Perhaps the ring had no meaning, or perhaps the meaning had been lost.

'What are you thinking?' Dhriti asked from her place across the table.

Prahlad shook his head. He was in his tent, having dinner. Today was supposed to be a cheery day.

It was the day truce had been declared. He had heard the whispers about Indra giving up and burst into delighted laughter. No more bloodshed. No more horrors and cries of any kind. It was over—finally.

'I am … I don't know.' For once, Prahlad was at a loss for words with the woman he loved.

Not one to take no for an answer, Dhriti dragged her chair closer to Prahlad's and sat down beside him. 'What is troubling you, my love?'

'You sound like an idiot.'

'That's what I was going for … idiot.'

Prahlad chuckled. 'I was thinking about whether I should meet Narasimha and speak to him about the truce. Nudge him towards the peace that it would bring to both sides.'

'You should. You two don't communicate.'

'Because he has alienated me. Not my fault.'

'You have grown distant too. You don't speak your mind now. It's your fault as much as his. I am sure he cares about your feelings.'

Prahlad nodded, though he didn't believe it. Dhriti was simply being nice, trying to smooth things between them, but Narasimha was an alien to him, a stranger. He changed tack. 'What are you thinking? Are you thinking about the marriage?'

'I am thinking of you right now.'

'You are a liar.'

'No, I am worried. Marriage can wait.'

'I don't know.' Prahlad sighed.

They had discussed the issue several times, but they had not arrived at a satisfactory conclusion even once. He was young and so was she, but royalty would marry around this time. Age wouldn't matter. They were adults in everyone's eyes and Dhriti, who had never given marriage a second thought, wanted to tie the knot. She was an orphan, and she had faced troubles for most of her life. But now she had Prahlad by her side, and she wanted them to be together forever.

Prahlad was hesitant, though. He wanted to get rid of all the worries that plagued him before he started a new chapter in his life. He frowned as he thought of the city and how unsettled everything was.

'You don't have to worry about this now. We will figure it out later.'

'But I want to be there for you. It's just that I am worried.' He clenched his fist. 'I don't know how things are right now and how bad they might get. I want to sort it out before—'

'Then do something about it,' she interrupted. 'Talk to him. Encourage him to accept the truce.'

Prahlad grimaced at the thought of what he had to do. But he didn't have a choice; he had been running away from a decent conversation for far too long. He sighed, sipped some water and nodded to himself.

I shall talk to Narasimha.

Prahlad and his guards had been waiting outside the royal tent for a while now. Though they were in their own war camp, everyone who was senior had personal protection on the off chance that there was an assassin in their midst.

People had entered the tent and exited. The night had shown its temper by letting loose an unexpected drizzle. And still Prahlad waited.

'His Highness has summoned you,' the guard finally said.

Prahlad nodded and entered the tent, leaving his guards outside. The interior reeked of wine and overripe fruits. He saw Narasimha sitting in his makeshift throne and sipping wine. He was alone. He had been alone for a while.

What was he making me wait for if there was no meeting?

Prahlad didn't bother asking him. The man was obviously drunk.

'Are you all right?' Prahlad asked. 'One of your celebration nights?'

'Indeed. What is happening, boy?' came the gruff response.

Narasimha sounded like his father. Cold. Distant. Even the space between them seemed to stretch endlessly. Prahlad rubbed the top of his ring, as if drawing strength from it.

'I heard about the truce. I was wondering what you're going to do about it.'

Narasimha growled under his breath and came to his feet unsteadily. 'Everyone is going on about the bloody truce. What is so great about it? A man giving up without a fight is no man for me.'

'So what are you going to do?'

'I do not know.'

Prahlad had expected this. Narasimha was not decisive, for he had no experience in statecraft. He had advisors, but they were just sycophants. Only Prahlad offered him the bitter truth and, for that, he received harsh coldness.

'You must have some idea.'

'What do you think I should do, commander?'

Commander … the name haunted him. He didn't want it, but it had been thrust upon him. He had never been interested in warfare, even though he had got considerably better at it.

'I believe you should accept it.'

'And what would I get?'

'Peace.'

'What about my vengeance? You don't care about Chenchen,' Narasimha blurted.

'I do.' Prahlad sighed. 'I do. I am … worried.' He shook his head. 'I don't want you to be blinded by vengeance like my father was.'

'I think it's the curse of the stead.' Narasimha laughed like a fool as he looked behind at the throne. 'It's the bloody stead,

I tell you. It holds this grand power within it that curses and tramples me into believing that I am doing the right thing by pushing for vengeance.'

Prahlad pursed his lips. 'There's still time to do the right thing. To be better than our enemies.'

'Indeed.' Nara threw the goblet on the floor. 'Or ...'

'Or?'

'I kill him. I attack him right now and I kill him. What should I do?'

Prahlad shook his head. 'That would be unwise.'

'We know how Indra is. How do you know this is not some trick he's playing on us?'

'Because his ego matters more than the tricks. He has given up and that is a big blow to his ego.'

Narasimha mulled over his words in silence and then began to hum the tune within him, beating his chest. 'It was a war chant. A chant to calm your nerves, to make you think carefully. It was taught to me when I was young, to make me feel sane. Now, it just makes my heart cry. Maybe it's because I am an old man or maybe because the circumstances are no longer the same.'

Prahlad came forward and knelt next to the man he considered his father, his friend. 'I firmly believe you should accept the truce.' He looked into Narasimha's eyes and smiled, enveloping him in the warmth he desperately needed. 'I believe you know just as I do that our kingdom requires peace more than warfare. Let's work at rebuilding our society, getting the starving masses off the streets, giving them shelter and providing them with bread and work.'

Prahlad saw the glint of the ring he wore on his hand. Narasimha nodded and wrapped him up in a drunken hug. For a moment, both of them felt the familiar comfort that had existed between them once.

'Fine. I'll do as you say,' Narasimha responded.

Prahlad had not experienced such hope in a long time.

CHAPTER NINE

There were moments when she would go back down memory lane and revisit past events. Like when her baby was snatched from her before her very eyes and she was left in the cold; her last glimpse of Bhringi.

This time it was something else, equally unpleasant but just as horrible.

She was back in the Gurukul, an orphan. She had just met Brahmani. She had stolen the spiritual guide, the *Manusmriti*, and was scolded for it, for it was not to be touched without the permission of the guru, especially by women. But she had wanted to gain knowledge. Besides, why was a folder filled with names tucked within the pages of the *Manusmriti*? Young though she was, she understood there was more than met the eye.

Parvati was sitting in front of the guru, her eyes filled with shame. 'I'm sorry, Guruji. I merely sought knowledge,' she said, glancing at him furtively.

Wisdom shone brightly in that deeply lined, wrinkled face. 'You don't understand, do you? You have broken a rule, and for that you must be punished—you must be cursed.'

Parvati was innocent. Until then she hadn't known what a curse was and what its implications were. But now she did. It was saying something foul with such sincerity that fate made sure it came to pass.

'You will always have problems with the people you love. You will never be able to touch them because they'll always go away from you. You will be their downfall.'

Parvati listened to these words and bowed her head, accepting the curse. Whether she deserved it or not was purely subjective, for there had been no malice in her actions. Regardless of the curse, she knew that she would reign one day.

And that day, women would be allowed to read the same texts as men.

Parvati's heart was racing and a million thoughts were running through her mind. She knew she was on the right path. There was a familiar chill in the air, as if awaiting her return; it was frightening. She thought about what had happened earlier. In a bid to quench his thirst for bloodshed, Andhaka had sent paid mercenaries to attack the Matrikas, but they had been unsuccessful. He had underestimated them—or perhaps he was simply trying to slow them down.

The Matrikas walked beside her, weapons at the ready, prepared for an attack. The night was bright—the moon was in its full glory, as if helping them find their way to their destination. The sound of dead leaves being crushed underfoot mingled with the noises of the night creatures hidden in the depths of the woods, away from prying eyes. She had heard about these creatures of legend often, especially while living in the north. They had dominated the forests before the war between the Devas and Asuras began. Some people believed they were victims of the war whose souls lived within the trees; they spoke through leaves and they killed intruders with their sharp branches and vines. Parvati had heard they could even shape-shift into gorgeous-looking creatures when they hunted.

Even though the Matrikas had grown up in woods, they felt a sense of unease that made the hair at the napes of their necks rise. Despite the chill in the air, beads of sweat appeared on their foreheads.

'Oh goodness!' shouted Chamundi.

Parvati turned and saw that the roots of a tree had grown long and twined around Chamundi's legs.

They stopped, realizing it had suddenly got darker. The moon was now hiding away from the growing branches of the trees that were trapping them all in.

Parvati was the first to attack. Raising her trident, she started striking at the roots that were tightening around her arms and legs, but every time they she managed to sever one, another would grow and ensnare her. Chamundi, by now, was hanging upside down, her legs in the grip of the evil roots.

Brahmani had had more success evading the roots than the rest. Her agility and speed had not let even one root touch her body.

'This technique is definitely not working, women,' Chamundi shouted, hacking at one of the roots.

'We need to think of something. This is never-ending,' screamed Parvati.

Suddenly, she realized that Narasimhi was unusually quiet. The other Matrika spent more time in the forest than any of the others. Parvati glanced around and realized that she was completely covered by the roots, yet she wasn't fighting back or even moving.

'Narasimhi, can you hear us?'

There was no reply.

'Narasimhi, please talk to us.'

Nothing.

The women were scared; their hearts were thundering. Parvati had a horrified look on her face. Sweat dripped from her forehead. She was cold and her skin prickled with fear. She could feel the will to fight slowly seep out of her. She had felt like this twice before. The first time was when her son was snatched away while she lay on the snow, alone and helpless. And the second time, when she had walked up to Chenchen, who lay on the ground with an arrow in her body, lifeless.

She could not lose anyone anymore. She needed to snap out of her thoughts and save her women. They were the last of her loved ones; she had already lost her son, her husband and her best friend—she couldn't lose anyone else.

I have to do this.

Parvati began to recall all the training she had received when she was growing up. How she had lived not as a queen, but as a pauper, a wine girl in one of the fancy kingdoms of the Asuras. How she had met a guru in one of the forests and sought knowledge from him. How she had met the rest of the Matrikas as a young girl and grown to like them. And how Indra had taken them … How she had met and fallen in love with Bhairav. She was just a young girl then, full of longing.

Parvati's mind raced through the crevices of history.

And then she remembered.

The vines! She knew what they were—and what to do! In one of the books at the Gurukul, she had read … oh, Narasimhi! They had read it together!

'Believe me when I say this. Act dead,' she told Brahmani, who was standing beside her.

'What do you mean?' Brahmani asked, slashing one of the vines, which had thorns.

'These trees—they have a consciousness, but they are not evil. They think we are evil because we are intruders. Act dead and let them retreat. When they do so, we shall make a run for it,' Parvati explained. 'That's what Narasimhi is doing. Acting dead.'

Since no other ideas were forthcoming, the Matrikas did as Parvati suggested and stopped resisting the vines. The moment they did so, the vines began to tighten around them. Moments passed …

And, as suddenly as they had attacked, the vines withdrew.

The instant they were free, Parvati shouted, 'MOVE!'

The Matrikas ran as one, only to stop at a village where the air was heavier and the stillness haunting.

They were camping, creating an outpost under the dark sky. The night was departing, making way for the sun. They were in the cold winters of the north, far from where they had started. Travelling to find Andhaka had been a challenge, a journey filled with adventures. Now, a resting period was necessary.

Parvati stared at the fading moon: it looked beautiful. Most of the Matrikas had gone to sleep around the warm fire. They had scouted the area before resting. There were no threats.

'Are you okay?' Brahmani asked, sitting next to her. She looked exhausted, but she spoke with a calm smile. 'Thanks for saving us back there.'

'Just waiting for the orange gleam,' Parvati answered, ignoring her thanks. They were a team.

'What are you thinking?'

'That I had no identity till my husband died.'

Brahmani looked down. 'What made you think that?'

'There's so much I had pushed down within me that I didn't even realize it. It was not Bhairav's fault. I was lucky to have such a wonderful man. It was just the way things were around me. I was in the house the whole day and I would weep. Whenever I tried to do something, the soldiers would come to help me. I was not a queen but brittle glass. Now, out in the open like this, I feel alive.'

'That's good to know. That's why our guru had told us, "Do not marry." For your focus would shift from saving the country from evil.'

'And yet he was against me touching books? What a hypocrite.'

'You never liked him.' Brahmani chuckled.

'No, it's just … in all aspects he wanted us to fare better than the opposite sex, but when it came to his faith—he would keep the men on top. Follow the old ways, he would say when it came to religion.' She pursed her lips. 'I wonder— did the people who made the old ways have the foresight for the new age?'

Brahmani raised her brows. 'Quite philosophical you have become.' She patted her on the back.

Parvati grinned. As they sat in comfortable silence, watching the sky, the day dawned, birds began to fly about and in the still weak light of the sun the snow didn't feel so cold any more.

For a moment it felt like home. And that was probably what Parvati needed.

'Nrriti,' she began, 'told me that Skanda wouldn't be the one we think he is. That he's an Asura.'

'Yes. It is Andhaka.'

'But Andhaka is not an Asura. He was brought up by one.'

'She didn't specify. So we don't know.'

'What if there is a Skanda and we don't know about it? What if he's still not corrupted?' Parvati asked.

'I don't think any of us had children except you, Parvati. So it wouldn't make sense.'

Parvati nodded. She was right. It had to be Andhaka. 'I suppose I just want to look at the world in a more hopeful way for now. I expected that by thinking that Skanda was alive, I would be able to avoid thinking that the world had got corrupted. Skanda being alive is a sign of hope.'

'I understand.'

'We think he's going to Hiranyaksha's land, Hiranyayetra.'

Parvati had heard about it. A land dedicated to worshipping Hiranyaksha, where the dead walked and the corpses still lay, where wild animals prowled, ready to devour you. She had never thought she would have to walk on those lands.

A chill went down her body.

'Do you fear the place?'

Parvati shook her head. 'No, but I fear the reason Andhaka is going back.' She looked at Brahmani. 'To the place he hated the most.'

CHAPTER TEN

At times Indra would delve into the past, searching for the day it had all started. It was a day he didn't regret. In fact, he cherished it, no matter how daunting it had been and how terribly afraid he had been.

He remembered the caves. The sound of the trickling water as the snow melted. The echoes of his breath and the strange dragon tree that rested. No sunlight had breached the walls and made its warmth felt here, yet the tree grew unchecked, with fireflies that lit up the place like lamps.

Indra was there. Young. Alone. Wearing a fur like a combatant's armour. His hair fell to his waist and his face was creaseless. He wasn't then the man he was today. He was the king of Amravati, the thunder god.

'Was I wrong to come here?' he called out. 'Or does the witch lady stay?'

There was a sudden gust of wind in that windless cave.

'Where are you, O goddess of death, who has stopped my daughter from living?' His face was drawn and filled with pain.

It was only a few months ago that he had noticed Jayanti's breathing was laboured. She would cough every now and again and sometimes throw up blood. It was clear that she was gravely ill. Indra had tried everything …

Except negotiating with the one who wanted to take her away.

Burning with hatred against Nrriti, he said, 'I heard that you have the power to hurt me, and I can't do anything about it. You control death. You control the afterlife. I am here to talk. To figure out a way. I can't bear to see my daughter, my child'—his voice broke—'in agony. Please, O mighty goddess, grant me a response.'

There was the wind again.

'Why are you doing this to me! Do you want the king of kings to beg you? Horrible, filthy woman!' Indra cursed. He couldn't control his temper any longer. The elephant sigil stitched on his cape glowered.

Your silence has more words than the venom that you spew.

'How are you doing this?' He frantically looked around, his blade glimmering in the dim cave. The voice was like a hiss, not a snake's but a widow's whisper. 'How dare you enter my mind, you filthy woman?'

You have come here for your dead daughter, yet you spout such obscenities.

'She's not dead!'

Not yet, my lord.

Indra growled and his fingers sparkled with powerful pulses of electricity. 'I shall burn the tree and see you burn as well if you don't show yourself.'

No need to see me, son of Kashyapa. Aren't you the one who was born penniless, a foreigner to the land of Illavarti, brought in by Sage Kashyapa and taught the ways of the skies, of thunder and bolts of lightning? You were taken in his arms and you were given his stead, just like your adopted brothers. Isn't it true?

His days as a child ... Indra chose not to remember them. There had been a lot of crying, a lot of scowls and a lot of worry, not to mention the horror of being tortured by his stepfather.

You and the Asuras ... you are no different. You were born with hate. All of you. And all of you think you understand Dharma.

'My brothers stand for what's right,' Indra said.

There was a chuckle of disbelief.

Kashyapa had a dream. To let the Devas rule the country of Illavarti. He loved your mother, Aditi, too much and when he saw you, he loved you even more. He began to hate the Asuras—his own sons. He despised and ostracized them from the world of Illavarti. Do you know why there will be endless wars between you? Because you are blood brothers. But there is a secret ... oooh ... a secret of great import.

Indra was silent.

The Asuras were born disfigured while the Devas were born with good looks—and were accepted. In the end, for Kashyapa, it was about how they looked.

*Imagine the horrors of the child. What … a … morose …
sight it would have been. Rejected by the ones who brought you
into the world.*

Indra had heard about it, but he didn't care. He didn't try to
argue. He and the Asuras might be stepbrothers, but he didn't
believe in it. He was a Deva. A pure breed. A descendant of
the Adityas, from Daksha's bloodline. He had heard some of
the rumours, but he dismissed them as hearsay.

Kashyapa had wanted a fierce republic in Illavarti and
thus, through the practice of niyog, he had planned to have
multiple races of children—only to fail when it came to the
Asuras.

Your arrogance will cost you a child.

'I want her to be saved. Tell me a way. There has to be a
way to cheat death.'

You don't cheat death. There was a giggle. *Death cheats you.*

Indra paused. This meaningless banter was getting him
nowhere. The wind blew again and his ears pricked.

*To save her, you must let go of the very thing that makes you
arrogant. Your power over the skies and thunder. The power to
summon Vajra.*

Indra laughed. 'That's impossible. Not to mention foolish.
I can't do that. My enemies will pounce on me.'

Then let your daughter die a painful death!

A chill went down his spine. 'Is there no other way?'

No. But your power will not leave you.

'What do you mean?'

*It will rest within her. Although, to get it back, you might
have to rip it out from her, literally claw through her skin, and
eat her heart and drink her blood. You may have to kill her to*

once again become the very arrogant man you are right now. To become the thunder god.

This was the most twisted surprise he had received. Indra licked his lips. 'If I let go … will she be okay?'

Yes. The reason she is the way she is is your karma. To overturn her fate, you are bending your own.

Indra had done horrible things. And nothing could redeem it. He sighed, looked down, unclasped his sword and let the blade fall to the ground. The sound of metal hitting rock echoed through the large cave.

'Fine. Fine. I—I get it. Let's do this.' He knew he had to save her. The consequences would be grave, but he loved his daughter too much.

And at that moment, as his wish came true, there were no storms in the skies. For the first time in many years, it had gone silent.

Indra stood in a corner respectfully, watching as Jayanti scribbled something on the sheets before her. Her relationship with the quill had begun as a young girl, when she would write down her thoughts. Now, things were different. Now she wrote stories and plays and poetry. Each more beautiful than the one before.

Indra glanced at the scroll in his hand. It was the reason he was here.

When he saw Jayanti pause, he walked towards her with a smile. 'Hello?'

No response.

'Are you talking to your old man?'

Jayanti looked up. Those crystal-grey eyes, so like his own, were a sign of the storms that resided in her. 'Depends. If he has screwed up something for good again.'

'I listened to you and I did it.' He showed her the scroll and gave it to her.

She rose to her feet. The morning's bright sunlight illuminated both their faces. 'What is it?' As she read it, her lips curved into a smile.

Indra cleared his throat to mask his embarrassment. He found himself feeling shaky and unsure before his domineering, confident daughter, but he loved her. Oh, he loved her too much. 'I asked for a truce and Narasimha has accepted it. We are going forward with it. We shall meet in the middle to finalize the arrangement. I have lost a lot, for sure, but I have gained something very important,' he said, his eyes on Jayanti.

She looked up questioningly, a half-smile still lingering on her face.

'I have gained that look.'

Jayanti beamed. 'You don't want to fight further?'

Indra shook his head. 'I'm done fighting.'

She couldn't believe she was hearing something like this from her own father. 'I hope you stay like this.'

'I will.'

'Are they coming in a convoy?'

'No, we are supposed to go. He has invited the family.' There was an unexpected quiver of fear in his voice. 'I know that it won't be trouble, but it would mean something. I know Narasimha. He has anger. A lot of it. But he's not a betrayer.

He won't stab me in the back,' he said, almost as if he was trying to reassure himself.

'Are you sure?'

'Yes.' Indra smiled. 'And I have to look for the best in people. Isn't that what you told me?'

Jayanti nodded. 'When you hear the stories of the nobles, you know that there are heroes. As a kid, I grew up reading about those heroes. I want my father to have that respect. I want the children of the future to hear tales of the great Indra.'

Indra didn't know when Jayanti had matured so much. 'I wanted that too. That is why I went through so much to conquer lands. That is why I fought and killed so many. But I realized over the years that you don't become a hero when you wield a sword. You become one when you choose not to lay one down.'

She smiled. 'I'm proud of you, Father.' And then she hugged him. An embrace tighter than ever. 'You should know though,' she whispered, 'that I know what I am and how I survived the horrible illness I had as a child. I hear people speak about it and I know that when I get angry, the ground shakes and the skies move.'

Indra froze. He couldn't believe that she was saying all of this while her arms were wrapped around his neck. He felt guilty for placing this burden on her, for not having told her. He wanted to explain himself, to justify his actions, but he kept silent as she continued.

'I also asked around and I won't name names, but I know that if you kill me, your power will be restored.' She pulled back. 'I pray that day never comes,' she said, her eyes filling with tears, 'but if it does and you find yourself at a disadvantage, do not hesitate. I will never hold it against you.'

'Don't speak like that. I would never do that in a million years.'

She nodded, tears in her eyes. 'And I wish that to be true. But if that moment comes, do not hesitate. Please. More than myself, I want you and Mother to be safe.'

Indra hugged her back wordlessly. Outside, the skies had turned grimmer than they were a few moments ago. Rain began pelting the earth.

CHAPTER ELEVEN

He knew what he had to do.

Garuda might not have been as affectionate as most Suparns were, but he definitely cared about others. Especially this kingdom. He wallowed in its glory because he sought comfort here. He knew he could bring about a change for the better. But then he was ostracized from his own home by Varuna …

He wanted a home. But after Varuna's death, Naaglok had become Indra's keep. It was the first thing the Deva had done to establish his maritime trade and naval supremacy. He had taken over after Hiranyakashyap's death too.

Garuda had no time to think these ill-thoughts. Killing Hiranyakashyap hadn't yielded him anything. Instead, it had made things more difficult and he had joined Narasimha. Even though the man was driven by vengeance, he believed in Narasimha and the way he looked at the world. Narasimha was an executioner. He got things done.

And he had. Slowly, but steadily, he had begun to take hold of the southern city of Kashyapuri and transformed it into a land for tribes other than the Asuras. Garuda liked it. He had always despised the Asuras. But then, as he knew first-hand, the Devas weren't too kind either. Whatever he planned, the home that he wanted to create, on his mother's grave, the life he imagined for himself, a woman, a child …

Would be taken away. All of it. By one insidious man—Vaashkal.

Garuda didn't trust the Asura. And he had shared this with his lady love, whom he was with—on the bed, his bronze body gleaming with sweat after passionate lovemaking.

'What are you thinking?' Sonapatra asked him.

He looked at her and noticed a slight scar. Sonapatra wasn't a Suparn, she was a Manav. But what a beauty she was. He had found her in the canteen of the camps and taken an instant liking to her. She was older but very attractive. There was something comforting about her. She reminded him of all the virtues and follies his mother had had and it made him feel more secure.

He smiled at her. 'I don't trust anyone here except for Nara.'

'And you shouldn't. Nara works on passion. Everyone else is playing some sort of selfish mind game.'

'Yes.'

'Come here.' She sat up against the bedstead and opened her arms. He lay his head on her bosom and wrapped his arms around her like an infant, even though he was twice as large as her. 'What are you thinking of doing?'

'Trespassing.'

'That's illegal.'

'Well, good thing I am the commander of the city.'

'Nara would expect you to be on the battlefield.'

'There's no battle. I returned because Nara declared truce and sent me back. He listened to Prahlad.'

'Do you think it was a wise move?'

'I don't know. I don't know what's right, but it's right for him. I was ready to claw Indra to death for killing his wife and taking his child from him.'

She played with his hair. 'Because you are a man of passion like him, which is why it is unlike him to do this.'

'I know. But it's a way of bidding goodbye. While I need to find out more about that bloody Vaashkal.'

She embraced him tightly and he remained there in the comfort of her arms, wondering how to bring about Vaashkal's downfall …

He was soaring in the skies.

He had to do more research. He had to find out who Vaashkal was. Who he had been in touch with. What he was up to. What he was thinking.

Drifting across the sky, he found himself in front of the keep that belonged to Vaashkal. Standing tall in a corner of the vast city, the keep was an imposing brick-and-mortar structure, surrounded by guards.

The very guards who had thrown him out just hours ago when he had presented himself at the gates with his band of Suparns and demanded entry.

'I would like to meet Vaashkal.'

The Asura soldier at the gate had said, 'Commander, he's at the war camps.'

'Not an issue. I'll meet his steward then. I have some political work to discuss.'

The soldier nodded and then went inside to ask the steward whether it would be possible. Garuda waited on his stallion, while the animal neighed and stomped on the earth with frustration under the hot sun. A few minutes later, he was admitted into the keep. As he walked through the halls with his men, he saw, right in the middle of the fort, a large garden enveloped in greenish fumes. There were plants of all kinds, some familiar, but most unfamiliar, and narrow paths between them for people to walk on.

'What is this?' he asked a soldier who was standing close to the garden.

'These are the master's prized possessions, the most poisonous plants known to mankind, planted and nurtured here, Commander.'

Garuda swallowed nervously. *This is a strange hobby for a man.*

After a while, the soldier who had gone to speak to the steward returned. His eyes were stark and grim, quite unfriendly. 'The steward is busy at the moment and chooses to meet when the master is present.'

'It's just a simple meeting, lad.' Garuda grinned disarmingly, but it failed to work on the soldier, who was staring at him with dead eyes.

'Unfortunately, I will have to ask you to leave.'

'I am the king's right-hand man,' Garuda growled under his breath, 'and I am being kicked out by a bloody steward.'

He didn't bother arguing with the guard and left.

But not really.

Moments later he was soaring in the skies, his wings outstretched, gliding effortlessly in the air. At the sight of the keep, he began to descend. He knew he had to enter Vaashkal's private study. He had anticipated being turned away when he had visited the keep earlier, but at least he now had a rough idea of the layout.

Garuda made his way to the window of what he assumed was Vaashkal's study and instantly let go of his wings, which continued to burst with energy and remained suspended in mid-air. He dove in through the opening and execute a perfect drop-and-roll …

Only to be seen by a scrawny old man sitting on a stool and scribbling on a piece of paper with his quill.

'I assume you are the steward.' Garuda grinned. He was wearing a cloak with the hood pulled down low over his face.

'Ah … ah …! Who are you! Gua—'

Garuda was beside him in a single stride. Covering his mouth, he pushed the steward against the wall. 'Don't say a word.'

There was a knock at the door.

'Are you all right, sir?' The knocking became louder.

'Just answer them calmly,' Garuda said, his face still hidden under the hood. 'Do you understand me?'

The steward instantly nodded, his eyes wide with shock.

Garuda slowly removed his hand. 'Say it,' he whispered. 'Speak or I shall kill you here.'

'I'M FINE! I'M FINE!' said the steward loudly. 'I just dropped something. It's fine, everything is fine.'

There was silence on the other side of the door. And then the soldier responded, 'All right, sir. Thank you.'

As the sound of footsteps faded away, Garuda looked back at the steward. 'Now, you are going to tell me everything about Vaashkal.'

'You might as well kill me,' the steward said and fell to the ground, unconscious.

Garuda stepped over him with a huff of disgust. *Well, I don't need him.* He went to the table and began to look through the scattered documents and pried into drawers. 'Come on, come on …' His eyes fell on a bunch of letters. Some were addressed to ministers, others were addressed to the people outside … And one—kept in an ornate box hidden under the table—from …

Garuda stared at the name in disbelief.

Hiranyakashyap.

'That's weird. Why would the earlier king address a letter to a petty moneylender like him?' he asked himself.

He began to read the letter. When he finished, he kept it back in the box. He was placing the box in its original position when the door burst open.

Alarmed, Garuda retreated, using his gauntlets to deflect the arrows being shot at him. Relying on the element of surprise, he slid across the floor towards the two guards in front and pulled out their swords to slash at them.

'INTRUDER! INTRUDER!' the guards shouted, sounding the alarm. Trumpets blared all over the keep, alerting the soldiers.

With heavily armed men rushing at him from both sides, Garuda took the only way out. He jumped off the balcony, narrowly escaping the arrows that were shot at him. A quick glance confirmed his suspicion—he was about to land right in the middle of the poison gardens. The moment his feet touched the pathway, he tucked himself into a ball and rolled on the ground to reduce the impact. When he got to his feet, he found himself at the intersection of the paths, with guards approaching him from all sides.

I think I'll have to fight my way out of this mess.

'What are you waiting for?' Garuda called out.

The soldiers took a few hesitant steps towards him, glancing warily at the plants on either side. Garuda launched himself at the closest soldier and pushed him into the fumes. The man fell on the ground, howling in pain, cradling his burning face in his palms. The other soldiers halted, seeing the state the man was in.

Garuda grinned at them and brandished his swords. 'Your fate will be the same if you come any closer.'

As the soldiers hung back, Garuda seized the opportunity and stormed their ranks, slashing at some, tossing some others into the poisonous fumes. He rushed upstairs to the study through which he had entered and barred the door against the fresh horde of enraged soldiers chasing him. He ran to the window …

Here goes nothing.

… and jumped.

Garuda managed to grab on to the wings that were still suspended in mid-air and somehow wore them. By the time the guards broke down the door and poured into the room, he had vanished in the skies.

As he soared upwards and watched the city of Kashyapuri become smaller and smaller, his thoughts cleared.

He finally had what he needed—leverage over Vaashkal, something Vaashkal would not want revealed.

That he, Vaashkal, was Hiranyakashyap's son—and brother to Prahlad.

CHAPTER TWELVE

Indra didn't know how to react.

He had brought his men closer to the fields where they were meeting, right in the heart of the war camp where the Chandals were going back and forth, carrying bodies ravaged by battle. The pungent, coppery smell of blood was all around. Silence reigned except for the sound of hoofbeats. The war camp that was chosen by Narasimha was filled with people, holding their torches and welcoming them. They had decided to meet in the middle and bring forth a hundred men each in what would be a peaceful transaction of faith.

Indra leapt down from his mare, and on the side he could see Jayanti, Sachi, Brihaspati and Vayu. They all were concerned, but Indra was confident. His eyes narrowed as took in the tents in the distance, secured with large nails.

The heavy silence was broken by a soft drumroll. Moments later, Narasimha appeared. He looked different from what Indra remembered, more regal. He was wearing his mane and

a crown on top of it, a golden dhoti like Hiranyakashyap's and
an angavastram over his shoulders. He was flanked by a curly
haired man on one side and Prahlad on the other. From afar,
both youths looked identical, with similar builds and golden
eyes Indra saw Narasimha and they both shared a frown and
a scowl. All the soldiers were quiet.

'Hello, Nara.' Indra came forward.

Narasimha's face was partially hidden by the mane. He
bowed and extended his arms.

Indra smiled and embraced him.

Old friends, allies, bitter enemies—they held on to each
other.

Prahlad had never been much of a dancer.

But he tried. For Dhriti. They skipped from one place to
another, moving their feet to the music. Fireflies flickered,
and the lamps grew bright. Tables were laden with food and
drink—roasted meats, heaps of delicious vegetables, carafes
of wine and other spirits. The evening was alive with sounds
of flute and drums and laughter and the clinking of goblets.

Prahlad was holding Dhriti by the waist; he whirled her
around and kissed her on the cheek. She was in a beautiful
sari and was gleaming with desire and hope.

'You did it,' she said, as he drew her closer. 'You solved it
between them.'

'I had to remind him who he used to be. How he used
to be.' Prahlad smiled, glancing at the high table where all
the nobles and ministers of the opposing factions sat, with
Narasimha and Indra beside each other.

Narasimha was drinking silently. Prahlad knew that it would be hard for Narasimha to accept Indra as his friend, that he wasn't able to digest it.

'I just hope he's fine. I'm worried for him,' Prahlad remarked thoughtfully.

'Look here.' Dhriti turned him to face her again. 'You are mine tonight, my love. We should be celebrating, not worrying. You were triumphant today. The goodwill of humanity won and that's a rare occurrence, so while you can ... dance!'

'Yeah, perhaps you are right.'

'*I am*. Kiss me.'

Prahlad blushed. 'Fine, if you say so.'

'If I say so? What do you mean by that? If I don't say it, you won't do it—is that it?'

'Uh, no, nothing like that.' He chuckled, pulled her closer and kissed her lingeringly. They smiled at each other. 'That was nice.'

Dhriti nodded. 'Yeah. I have become so much saner ever since you've come into my life.'

All of a sudden, the music became louder and the dancing more enthusiastic. Prahlad began to say something, when his eyes fell on the high table again.

Narasimha was missing.

Indra had observed Narasimha leave the room. He wondered where Nara had disappeared to and why. His eyes met those of Jayanti, who seemed equally concerned, but before he could contemplate it further, Vaashkal, the minister of money next to him, asked, 'How does it feel to join hands?'

Indra ignored the question. Instead he gave a pointed look to the empty chair beside him and said, 'Whatever happened to him?'

'Oh, he's got a bad stomach.' Vaashkal grinned. 'I noticed your glass is empty. Let me pour some for you, my lord,' he said.

As Indra sipped the sweet wine, he said, 'I see. I hope it was his own decision—the truce, I mean.'

'Of course, my lord, it was. King Narasimha made the decision all by himself, regardless of what was told to him.'

'What do you mean?'

'He wanted to kill you and your entire family, but Prahlad, sweet boy that he is, stopped him from doing so. What a sad poor sap.' Vaashkal clinked his goblet with Indra's. 'Cheers to the truce.'

Indra didn't bother rising to the bait. 'We need to discuss a lot. Taxes. Incomes. Exports. What is mine and what is his ...'

'And you shall. With me. King Narasimha doesn't care.'

Oh for goodness' sake! KING Narasimha. Indra frowned. 'I knew him as a solider. *My* soldier, and now I am begging for his attention.'

'The tables have been turned, my lord.' Vaashkal smiled. 'You know, I have a beautiful poison garden. I would love to show it to you sometime.'

'I don't think Narasimha is happy.'

'There,' Vaashkal began, 'is a Venus flytrap. I don't know if you have heard of that sort of a plant. Quite a phenomenon it is. It has long fang-like mouth ... and it bites. Very interesting.'

'I don't understand.' Indra narrowed his eyes. 'Why are you telling me this story?'

'Oh, no reason. Just making conversation. I find plants fascinating. You see, the Venus flytrap swallows creatures that provide it with nutrition. It bites and sucks the life out of them. But the most interesting thing about it is that it appears to be completely harmless. Like an open tapestry for people to come and rejoice before, not realizing how dangerous it is.' Vaashkal's eyes turned grim and a note of callousness entered his voice. 'And the moment the fly sits on it and begins to feast on its juices, the plant traps it and kills it. Now the question in all of this is—was it the flytrap's fault that it killed the fly or the fly's for being careless?'

Indra sighed. 'I am not here to listen to your story. I am leaving. I need to meet Nara and sort things out.' As he rose, Vaashkal grabbed his hand.

'I would prefer it if you started believing that stories hold the power to frighten you more than the fright itself.'

'Something is wrong,' Prahlad said. He could see that Indra had left, while Vaashkal was busy drinking. 'Something is definitely wrong. I don't like this.'

'What happened?' Dhriti asked.

'It just doesn't feel right. I should follow them both.'

'But …'

Prahlad looked into her eyes and found comfort, though he knew that she was naive and indifferent to the situation. One of the passing waiters offered him some liquor, which he refused, his attention caught by the soldiers around him.

'Dhriti,' he said with a gasp. 'Why are our soldiers thinner than usual? They look so feeble. And tired.'

'I … I …' Dhriti turned around and noticed the oversized armour on some of the men nearby. 'I don't know. Why would they—'

'Because they are not our soldiers,' Prahlad answered grimly. 'They are not from our side. They must have been paid to be here.'

'What do you mean?'

Prahlad looked in her eyes; his own were worried and unsettled. 'They are a decoy.'

Indra entered the massive tent that belonged to the great King Narasimha. The man he had lived and breathed with in his youth. Still in his mane, Narasimha stood behind the throne, staring into the distance.

'Are you all right, Nara?' Indra asked softly. 'Why did you leave?'

Silence.

'I did not know it was her,' Indra said. 'I did not know she was with the Matrikas. I intended to kill only them. If I had known …' He shook his head. 'I would have never done it if I had known.'

'You are lying!' came the angry response.

'No, I am not.' Indra blinked. 'I might be savage, but I'm not heartless. I know the limits, my limits.'

Nara looked up at him. 'She was pregnant.'

Indra's heart sank. He hadn't known. Truly. And for some reason, he desperately wanted Nara to know that. 'You were always my friend before my soldier. Please try to understand. I did what I did because I was ...'

'You are still lying. Andhaka told you that Chenchen was with them. You sought vengeance.' Narasimha walked around the table, his gaze fierce, as if it could pierce through to Indra's soul. 'That's why you went there to kill them. Admit it! For the sake of this truce if for nothing else, admit that you knew'— he stopped a few feet from Indra and stared at him in the dim light of the tent—'and I shall forgive you.'

Indra looked at him. He was tearing up. The man was broken and destroyed. He hadn't imagined that Nara had loved Chenchen so dearly ... and the child ... Guilt washed over Indra.

'I am sorry.' He looked down. 'You ... are ... you are right. I knew. But I didn't know ... about the child. I swear I didn't.'

'And if you had? Would you have spared her life??'

'Perhaps not. I was a man bent on vengeance and there's nothing I can do about it now.'

'You can,' Nara said softly.

'What?'

'Swear.'

'I just did.'

'No.' He shook his head. 'Swear on your daughter's life.'

'I ...' Indra was confused.

But not for long. Moments later, he saw one of Narasimha's soldiers drag someone into the tent at knifepoint. Confusion gave way to shock and horror.

Jayanti!

All of a sudden, Asura guards burst upon the gathering and attacked Indra's soldiers while setting the tent ablaze. In a flash, Prahlad understood what was happening. He instantly grabbed hold of Dhriti, moved towards the high table and crouched underneath it.

Sachi, Indra's wife, was yelling, 'Where's Jayanti? Where's Jayanti?'

'We must leave, Sachi,' Vayu urged. 'Before the fire burns us.'

Shocked, Prahlad watched the soldiers tear each other down. *This smells like Vaashkal's ploy.* Vaashkal had brought civilians dressed as soldiers, decoys, to the truce negotiations, leaving the real Asura soldiers behind at their camp—except for the small group that had followed them and was now attacking Indra's men.

'What is going on?'

'Betrayal,' Prahlad said. 'We must make a move.'

Fire had engulfed the tent; flames licked at their feet and there was smoke all around them. The instant they emerged from under the table, one of Indra's men slashed at them with his sword. Dhriti whirled and struck the soldier with a high flying-kick aimed at his head. The soldier crumpled to the ground in an unconscious heap. Prahlad went for the man's sword while Dhriti grabbed that of another fallen soldier nearby.

'Get them!' A couple of Indra's soldiers had just killed a bunch of the decoy soldiers and were now focused on Dhriti and Prahlad. The men were standing between them and the door.

'You take the one on the left and I'll take the one on the right,' Prahlad said.

Dhriti didn't wait—she rushed forward and, with a mighty swing, beheaded one and impaled the other.

'Or'—she winked—'perhaps I take both.'

'Don't do this,' Indra pleaded.

But it was too late. The Asura held the knife close to Jayanti's throat, right next to her skin, and even if Indra flinched, he would not be able to save her.

'I have burned down your tent. All your prestigious ministers and nobles and family are burning to death as we speak,' Narasimha gloated. 'What a sight that must be. I'm missing it, but I have no regrets; I love what I'm looking at now.'

'Don't do this.' Indra was burning with hatred. He refused to believe that his family had perished, his men … No, they must have managed to escape. He was sure. They were not idiots. Vayu must have called the winds to cull the fire, even though he had problems handling it sometimes. 'What do you want from me?'

Narasimha came close to the frightened Jayanti, who was tearing up and calling out to her father, whispering his name and begging him to do something. 'You don't understand—I don't want anything from you. I just wanted to see you like this and exact my vengeance, once and for all.'

'Letting vengeance into your political objectives—you are an idiot. You will spoil things. You can still go back.'

Nara growled menacingly. 'No, I can't! I have nowhere to go back to, I have no one. Not since you killed my child and my love.' He raised his hands and, instead of letting the knife do the job, ripped Jayanti's throat with his claws.

The skies changed and Indra's heart sank. He tried to go to his daughter, but the guard came from behind and restrained him. Narasimha watched Jayanti bleed to death, then knelt beside her and tasted her blood. As Indra looked on helplessly, Nara slashed open her chest and crushed her still-beating heart in his massive hand. He could feel the currents in her body generate a strange power …

Suddenly there was a bright flash of light.

Indra was blinded for a moment. Realizing that he wasn't being held down any more, he started walking, fumbling in the darkness, until he tripped over something. When his sight was restored, he looked around the tent—it was empty. He had tripped over …

His daughter's body.

Tears trickled down his face as he gathered the corpse and held it to his chest. 'Please! Please, no … you can't do this. You promised, Nrriti. You promised you wouldn't take her!' He growled and clenched his teeth in frustration.

But his cries went unheard.

Prahlad watched from outside, frozen in anguish, helpless. He didn't know what to do and it broke his heart. There was a soft touch on his shoulder.

'He … he … he killed Indra's daughter.' Prahlad couldn't believe what had happened.

'No!' Dhriti gasped. They stood in silence for a few moments. All around them the tents were on fire, except for the one Indra was in. Smoke billowed into the night sky; an orange glow suffused everything. She took his hand and slowly led him towards the mare she had managed to steal from one of the soldiers. 'We must leave,' she said gently.

Prahlad followed her with leaden steps. He knew that if he lingered he would get caught. He was an Asura after all—Narasimha's man even though he no longer believed in what his leader was doing. As he climbed on to the mare's back, he wondered how he would ever forgive Narasimha for this betrayal. But, more than that, whether he would ever forget Indra's face. He had heard tales about Indra's savagery and ruthlessness, yet the person he had just seen clasping his daughter's corpse to his chest had been nothing more than a broken shell of a man.

Prahlad knew one thing for sure now. It was something he had considered before, too, but never acted upon. But now …

He would have to stop the tyranny of Narasimha.

He would have to vanquish the very man he had helped crown.

CHAPTER THIRTEEN

Death has a different smell, taste and sensation.

Parvati could feel that.

Evading death had become child's play for the Matrikas since they had embarked on this journey. They had been travelling on foot for almost a week now, stopping only to rest and catch up on some sleep. Occasionally, when she stood guard while the other women slept, Parvati saw a black raven circling them high above in the sky and flying away.

She knew what this meant.

Andhaka was watching. He routinely used ravens to track his enemies. The birds had been following them all along; he would know they were on their way.

As they continued on the last leg of their journey, Parvati noticed something strange about the place they were passing through. There were dead trees all around. Here and there vultures fed on the carcasses of snow leopards and other animals. An eerie silence pervaded the air. The town was situated at the foot of some hills, but there were no people who could tell them if they were on the right path. They walked on in search of some signs of life, some travelling over the cleft to see the cold waters.

'I don't see anyone. We entered the town almost ten hours ago,' Narasimhi said.

'There are houses and shops, but all of them are shut.' Trident in hand, Chamundi walked ahead of the group. She could taste the pungent air on her tongue.

The Matrikas had no clue as to what the place was called or which part of the world they were in; the only thing they could rely on was the trail in front of them. As night took over, the temperature dropped suddenly. It was the coldest Parvati had been since leaving her home in the north, but she soldiered on, encouraged by the thought that she was nearing her target. As Parvati and the other women walked, they heard a noise coming from deep inside the forest beside the abandoned city.

They decided to follow it.

After walking for several minutes, the Matrikas came upon a clearing in the heart of the forest. Some twenty or so wood-and-mud huts stood in the distance. People were milling about outside, some clustered around small bonfires while others sat at a table that could easily seat fifty people. At the sound of the Matrikas' approach, the residents drew their weapons and let loose a volley of arrows. The Matrikas took cover behind the trees at the edge of the clearing and waited out the attack, but they did not launch a counter-attack. They needed these people to tell them about the abandoned town.

'We come in peace,' Brahmani called out.

The tribespeople remained silent, watchful and wary of the strangers. Many minutes later, they stepped into the clearing, weapons at the ready in case of a surprise attack.

To Parvati's surprise, their attackers were scantily clad in animal skins and their bodies were adorned by symbols and signs. What disturbed her was how sickly thin each person was—their bones were jutting out, the jaws were prominent, the cheeks were hollow and the eyes had sunk deep in their sockets. It looked as if none of them had had a proper meal in ages, no more than the little needed to keep them alive.

'I am Brahmani, these are my friends.' Brahmani introduced each one by name.

A man with long white hair and ashen skin came forward. Parvati could see his eyes were young, but the lack of nourishment made him look decades older.

'I am Swapan, the chief of Hiranyakasipu.'

Hiranyakasipu, the city of the dead.

Parvati finally realized who the tribespeople were: they were not ordinary beings; they were the children of the dead, the Vaitarli.

She had heard about them before. Born from the hair of Shankar, the Vaitarli were dead, immortal beings. They usually kept to themselves and were hard to locate in any of the major cities of the region.

They fought for no one, supported no one, choosing to spend their immortality residing in and protecting the jungles. Anyone could turn into a Vaitarli with a special ritual of immortality.

'The city outside, what happened to it?'

'We were Manavs before tyrants in the form of crowned kings came. The ancestral home of King Hiranyaksha was hidden in the other corner of Hiranyakasipu. We were brought from the north to protect the king's lair. He offered us money and food. The only condition was that we would have to perform a yagna.'

Swapan continued, 'After the yagna, things started to change. Our bodies began hollowing out, we never felt hungry, couldn't sleep at night. Years passed, but we remained the same—our children did not grow, the adults did not age. That's when we learnt what the king had plotted. We cannot leave now—the conditions of the outer world are too harsh for us, we will be killed.'

'But then, why hide here and not live there?'

'After the death of the king, no one visited for years. We existed in peace. Our kind don't need food to survive. We never had the need to leave, until—'

'Until?' Parvati asked, turning around to look at Swapan.

'Until someone returned to the palace.'

'Who?'

'The prince who grew up here.'

The Matrikas left the Vaitarli soon after, on a quest to discover the secrets of the place. The closer they got to it, the thicker the air around them became. Parvati's senses were alert, she could feel the palpitations inside her chest. The son she had loved so dearly and lost in the crisis of war was so close. Her heart felt heavy knowing why she had taken this journey to find him: she would have to kill with her own hands the boy she had promised to protect.

She would not wish such pain on anyone.

The house was on its last legs; parts of the roof were hanging low, almost ready to collapse. The only thing that kept it upright were the seven pillars, six on each side and one in the middle. In the dark night, with the light of the full moon shining over it, the red façade glowed eerily.

Parvati entered the house with much caution, followed by the other Matrikas. All of them had their weapons drawn. They trod lightly, making no sound at all.

'You're finally here'—a screeching, high-pitched voice echoed in the main hall.

The Matrikas stopped walking and quickly got into formation, covering each other, ready to attack. Suddenly a flock of ravens flew in through the door behind them and perched on the carved handrail of the stairs. The door closed with a loud thud.

They had been locked in.

Parvati could see the silhouette of a man at the top of the stairs. Though it was dark and his face was hidden, she knew who it was. Their quarry, the person they had been chasing for so long.

Andhaka.

'It didn't take you long to find me,' he said, laughing as he emerged from the shadows and revealing his white skull and a red bandana across his eyes. He was so pale and sickly that it almost made Parvati's maternal instincts kick in; she wanted to scold him and tell him to eat nutritious food.

He continued, 'I was waiting for you ladies. I've been alone here for a long time.'

Parvati wanted to run to him and end the story here, but she looked around and gasped. They were surrounded by a group of the same Vaitarli they had met just hours ago, only now they were all smiling mysteriously.

Chamundi didn't wait; she plunged her trident into the woman next to her, but no blood poured out. The wounds healed as soon as she withdrew the weapon.

'The Vaitarli work for me. Their souls are bound to this place, making them loyal to the king alone. Seeing how long you fools were taking, I told them to help you along. I don't have time to waste,' Andhaka said. 'Finish them off,' he instructed the Vaitarli and started walking back to his chambers. 'I have work to do.'

Any resistance the Matrikas put up was of no use. In no time at all, they were each tied to a pillar in the great hall. The Vaitarli circled them, their eyes shining with hunger.

'We lied about our food,' Swapan said to Parvati, baring his teeth in a menacing smile. 'We eat the living.'

CHAPTER FOURTEEN

Prahlad was watching the waves crash against the heavy boulders ringing his fort. It stood on the edge of the ocean. On most days the beautiful view—the endless horizon, the fading sun and the seagulls that fluttered across the sky—had an uplifting effect on his mood. Today, though, he was solemn. Quiet. He was prepared. He had worn his breeches and kurta with a long sherwani and swept back his hair. His eyes were dark, like the light that had died in front of him. His breathing was slow. He was quietly murmuring to himself, preparing his speech.

After the massacre at the truce meeting, Indra's army had retreated instead of fighting further. Over the next fortnight, Vaashkal had sent emissaries all over the countryside, proclaiming that the lands and villages, the harvest and taxes that had been Indra's now belonged to Narasimha. In a few short weeks, Kashyapuri's domain had nearly doubled. Only

Amravati remained Indra's, but soon even that would be taken away, judging by the way things were going.

Throughout, Narasimha had been silent, absent. The rumours said he had fallen ill, was becoming mad. Prahlad dismissed the latter theory as soon as he heard it; Narasimha was already mad.

Prahlad was alone in his study, illuminated by the flickering light of a lamp in a corner. *Am I ready? To deceive? To usurp? To betray? To do it again?*

He was rubbing the ring of Shrivatsa. *Lord Vishnu, if there is hope, enlighten me. Show me the way and I shall abandon my plan.*

But nothing happened. Lightning didn't strike. The sky remained the same. And the ravens had been clawing through the clouds, hovering over the fort like a tarot reader's omen.

As he was about to walk out, he saw the letter he had written and rewritten multiple times—about summoning everyone to a discussion on important, discreet matters. It was supposed to be sent to the council of ministers from all domains. This information was not supposed to be shared with anyone, though Prahlad knew that it would be known to Narasimha.

But by then the decision would have been taken.

There was a firm knock at the door. Before Prahlad could say anything, the visitor entered.

'I heard what happened.'

Garuda.

'Hello.' Prahlad smiled weakly.

Garuda had saved him when his father had ambushed them back at the war camp that belonged to the rebels. Even without his gear, he seemed stern and imposing. 'My men told me a council is happening. What are you up to?'

'As prime minister, can I not call a meeting?'

'You can do whatever you want, as long as it benefits the kingdom.'

'And thus the meeting.'

Garuda said gravely, 'I have been on an investigation of my own, lad. And I'm learning things that are not in Nara's favour. He is at threat.'

Yes, he is. From me.

'I didn't know who to come to. I assumed you would be the best person to talk to. I have tried approaching him, but since the Burning of the Truce—that's what people are calling it apparently—he's not been himself. He has locked himself away. I heard he killed Indra's daughter and absorbed the power of thunder. I don't know what made him do that, but he's in trouble for sure …'

'That doesn't justify killing a young girl.'

Garuda frowned. 'I do not know what's right and wrong anymore.'

Prahlad nodded. 'What have you heard about these insidious plots against Nara?'

'I—'

He was interrupted by a knock at the door. A soldier stood outside. 'My lord, they are waiting.'

Prahlad dismissed him with a nod. 'Let's talk later.' As he moved past Garuda, the latter grabbed his arm.

'Don't trust anyone,' he cautioned.

Prahlad nodded again. He knew that warning would be more useful to Narasimha than anyone else right now.

The hall was bursting with people when Prahlad entered. The ministers of the Manavs, Asuras, Yakshas, Nagas and other clans were exchanging confused glances, wondering why they had been summoned this time, and in such haste. As Prahlad waited for them to take their seats, his eyes fell on the person who had just entered the room and widened in disbelief.

Vaashkal.

'I think you forgot to invite your minister of coin. I had to snatch the invitation from one of your runners.' Vaashkal shrugged. 'But I'm glad I'm here.'

Vaashkal was a loyalist. Prahlad considered aborting his plan, but if the decision was made immediately, then Vaashkal would be not able to do anything.

Prahlad walked to the centre of the hall. 'I have summoned you here to discuss something which we have all noticed but not spoken about.'

His words were greeted with silence.

'After we … rather I … killed my father, Hiranyakashyap, we had decided to build a state of democracy, of peace,' Prahlad continued. 'Yet here we are, waging wars once more. For a city which is already losing a lot of resources and money, squandering more on the army and consignments of mercenaries so we can continue to pillage and fight does not seem prudent.' He shook his head. 'We are not ready to go into battle again—'

'We don't have to,' Vaashkal interrupted. 'As you all know,' he announced when Prahlad turned to him with a frown, 'we won the war, a fact that our dear prime minister seems to have forgotten. Did the orange flames singe your memory, my lord?'

'I remember it clearly. But we need a leader who understands statecraft, not just battle.'

Vaashkal smiled grimly. 'What we need is an effective ruler. And Narasimha is one. What you are doing is beginning to look a lot like treason, my lord. I have been kind enough to not let you continue—if you do, the guards will turn on you.'

'Let them!' Prahlad snapped angrily. 'I have been to prison enough times to know that we don't need tyranny in a city which has already fallen once because of it. Our kingdom needs stability, peace, rebuilding … progress! When has a country ever been more about war and less about its people? Why do we let a few people's egos control the entire nation?'

Prahlad shook his head. 'Yes, King Narasimha won the war. He defeated the evil Indra. And the young woman who was killed—what about her? How can the king justify killing her?' He paused, watching people around him murmuring and mumbling in confusion. 'I am not saying Lord Narasimha is a dishonourable king. He is not. He's righteous and he works on something that no other ruler has: instinct. But his mind is being poisoned'—he glanced at Vaashkal—'and a ruler who succumbs to such trickery is not one who should be put on the throne. Thus have I come here, with the blood of the Asuras in my veins but belief in Lord Vishnu in my heart, to entreat you. We must compel the king to relinquish the throne and give it to someone else.'

'And who might that be?' one of the ministers asked. 'You were the one who supported Lord Narasimha, who insisted on electing him instead of you. You forfeited the right to kingship to give it to him even though, by the laws of the state, the oldest son inherits the throne. And now you come here, saying you have changed your mind!'

'I was naive and probably too hopeful.' Prahlad shook his head. 'I shouldn't blame it on my age; I wanted to be right.' His voice trembled. 'I wanted him to run the state because I believed he would do it better than I would have. But I was wrong. He can't. Now, as the council, only you have the power to displace him. To pull him down.'

Vaashkal got to his feet and addressed the crowd. 'Whatever decision you take, leave me out of it, but I promise you one thing—the man you are planning to depose is the same man who now holds the power of Vajra within his blood. He won't send his men to kill any of you for treason— he will come himself.'

The assembled ministers and chiefs began speaking in low murmurs. Fear engulfed them. Watching them, Prahlad felt defeated. He didn't want things to end this way.

'Who will be the king, though?' one of the ministers asked at last.

Prahlad blinked. 'I want to follow my father.'

The council members were taken aback. Prahlad waited in a corner while the ministers deliberated among themselves. Once before, when he had called a similar meeting to convince them to choose Narasimha as the king, they had followed his lead and agreed with him. *Would that still be the case?* He noticed Vaashkal sneering at him, but before he could wonder why, the council members came and settled back into their chairs.

'We have come to a decision unanimously.'

Prahlad waited.

'He stays, Prime Minister Prahlad,' the minister said. 'Narasimha stays king.'

CHAPTER FIFTEEN

'You have done what you wanted to do.'

Narasimha was back here again, the place where he always found comfort, but also this unsettling feeling of nausea. He was standing in the bay, its black waters glimmering in the moonlight.

'Where am I?' he asked himself. There was someone else in the water with him. He turned to see who it was. 'My love,' he said, gazing upon the familiar face.

She ignored his greeting. 'You have done what you intended. You made him suffer as you did when you lost me,' she said with cold eyes.

'Yes.'

'How does it feel?'

Nara didn't know. He felt a lot of things, but was triumph one of them, he wondered. Rather than answer that, he asked, 'Aren't you happy? Aren't you satisfied?'

'You say that as if you did it for me.'

'I did.'

'You killed a little girl for me?' She raised her brows. 'Interesting, how the blame is on me.'

Nara should have felt guilty, but there was too much bitterness in his heart. 'No matter what you say, my love, he deserved it.'

'And now what? Kill him too?'

He nodded. 'Eventually. But for now, I want him to live with regret and pain.'

'And afterwards?'

'What do you mean?'

'Once you kill him, what is your purpose?'

'I don't know.' He shook his head. 'I'll probably come to you.'

'But you don't deserve to be with me any more.'

Narasimha narrowed his gaze. All his life, he had felt he was a murderer, a horrible person, a plunderer. He had been a mercenary when he was in Indra's army. 'Oh, so when I did it earlier, for others, it was all right. But now, when I do it for myself, I'm wrong?'

'You were seeking redemption when you met me. Now you seek carnage,' Chechen said. 'And when you seek carnage, you become a victim of it. I told you: I see you in the fields, lying on the ground, a dagger in your heart, your life ebbing away. The only thing that would be worth dying for is me … but now, I won't be waiting for you.'

As she turned to leave, Narasimha tried to grab her. But it was no use. She slipped through his grasp like a wisp of air.

'No, don't go!'

'I'm but a memory … of a broken man.'

'No, you are more than that. You continue to be a memory here.'

She turned back. The water shimmered as she knelt and brought a drop of water against her cheeks, smiling as she did so. 'Did we have dreams, Nara? Did we dream to ever drown in our wonders?'

'What are you trying to say?'

'Whatever happened to that man who had so many dreams? Does he still dream? Have you fallen in love again?'

'No. Nor am I going to.'

'You need to move on. It'll be a year soon. Longer than we were together, actually.' She began to walk away. Nara went after her until she said, 'Where I go, you cannot follow. Your body, your blood—they are tainted.'

And then she disappeared, leaving behind the broken man that he was.

Narasimha was severely ill for nearly two weeks after drinking the blood of the girl. He was told he'd be ill, but he still did it. He was feverish and suffered bouts of delirium. When his fever finally broke on the fourteenth day, he was visited by the man who had become an unlikely ally and advisor: Vaashkal.

Still weak, Narasimha shuffled towards a long table at one end of the room and poured himself wine. The effort left him sweaty and exhausted.

'What are you doing here?' he rasped.

'Oh, nothing. May I sit, my lord?'

'Why are you so happy?' Nara scowled at the grinning Vaashkal.

'I had a fantastic night, that's why.'

'Your exploits in the brothels are quite well known. No need to gloat about them.' He sipped the wine. It tasted different.

Vaashkal's grin disappeared. 'Do you feel powerful?'

'I feel nothing. I don't think she had any Vajra in her.' He was feeling horrible, feeble, helpless … But the drink—he took another sip—it was helping him. 'Could it be that you are wrong?'

'No,' Vaashkal said firmly. 'We should try them, your newfound powers.'

'There are *no* powers!'

'Not yet. But if you exercise your muscles, I'm sure you will find them within you. You didn't know you were an Avatar either until you actually needed the powers, right?'

Narasimha nodded. 'All right, we can test it. But really, what is the purpose? I plan to sleep and not worry about the council or the state.'

'You should worry,' Vaashkal said.

'Why?'

'Prahlad was moving the council towards deposing you … tsk, tsk.' He shook his head.

For a moment, Narasimha couldn't believe his ears. He was befuddled. 'What?'

'He was urging the council to get rid of you, but as I'd anticipated, they voted for you. Everyone's scared, after all. What you pulled at the Burning of the Truce—people respect you for it … or they fear you, it's all the same. They wouldn't dare go against you.'

'Prahlad went against me?' Narasimha could not move past that bit of information.

'Yes. I'm sorry he turned on you. But don't forget, he's still Hiranyakashyap's ...' Vaashkal trailed off as he glanced out of the window.

Outside, the brightly shining full moon had turned blurry, storm clouds had gathered in the night sky and there was a loud crash of thunder. The weather had changed drastically in just a matter of minutes. Vaashkal quickly turned around and looked at Nara. The king was motionless save for the angry flaring of his nostrils. His rage, however, was palpable. It seemed to be seeping out of his body. Suddenly his fingers began to crackle with energy, and he flung a bolt of lightning across the room, smashing the bed in half. When the dust settled, there was a large mark across the wall in the shape of a thunderbolt.

'And you said you don't have your powers yet!' Vaashkal exclaimed with a large grin. 'Ladies and gentlemen, I present to you the wielder of Vajra—Narasimha.'

Nara had witnessed the immense power of the Vajra while he was serving Indra. It had made Indra invincible. He could perform miracles, bring down the skies, force lightning from the clouds ... or end dynasties and raze cities to rubble—all with a mere gesture. Any man whom Indra touched would suffer untold agony—his body would be flooded by cancerous cells and his mind plagued by frightening visions, leading to a slow and painful death. This was the power of Vajra, and the fact that he had it within himself astounded Nara. At this point, he didn't care much about how he had come to possess this power—rather, he felt that he deserved it.

'I want you to tell me what all happened,' he said through clenched teeth.

Vaashkal observed the dark smoke swirling around Nara and the sparks of lightning emanating from his fingertips with a mix of fear and amusement, and hastily complied. As he listened to Vaashkal, Nara's anger mounted. It was the same anger he had felt when Indra had embraced him and tried to act as if everything between them was all right, when he had killed Indra's daughter ...

Anger capable of decimating empires and killing thousands.

'Now if you are thinking of imprisoning him or killing him, I would say that's a fool's way of looking at it.'

'What do you mean?'

'He's the former king's son. If you do not want the wrath of the Asuras on you, you should not kill him. You can exile him somewhere so he's not much of a bother. Far enough from here, where he's not a menace who can try to influence the council. What do you think?'

'I want to talk to him.'

'Talking will lead to bigger problems. Get rid of him. Shoo him away. Let him know that you are angry so he doesn't dare cross you again. I'm worried if you see him, you might choke him.'

Narasimha shook his head. 'I made a promise a long time ago to protect him no matter what. And I have done so ever since. But he can't force my hand like this.'

'He's just worried for you, Your Highness. I just believe he needs some time off, to see other parts of the world with his wife.'

Nara nodded. Vaashkal was right. Though his rage had calmed, he still felt betrayed. 'I'll do what's necessary.'

'What does that mean?'

'You don't have to know everything,' he said sharply. 'Your exceedingly grateful attitude is quite alarming.'

'I serve the throne and the man ... correction ... the god who sits on it.' He winked and walked out, leaving Nara to his thoughts.

Nara struggled with the knowledge that Prahlad had betrayed him. He wanted to kill the boy, but he couldn't. He had been ignoring Prahlad for a while because he was too moralistic for Nara, but perhaps it was time to confront him. As he looked at the ring, the very same one that Prahlad also had, the one Nara had made for him, a thought slowly started to take shape in his mind ...

I need to get rid of him.

CHAPTER SIXTEEN

'I believe we have a problem.'

Vayu, Sachi and Brihaspati were gathered around a table, their tense, drawn faces illuminated by a dim light. They all respected and adored Indra, but right now they were all avoiding him. They were all back in Amravati, their kingdom. They had retreated from the attack at the truce meet and travelled hundreds and thousands of miles to return to the comfort of the familiar. At first, when they learnt Nara had killed Jayanti, they had decided to retaliate, but seeing their king and queen helpless and sobbing, they chose to withdraw. To preserve stocks, supplies and energies and go home. Gather reinforcements, hire mercenaries if needed, build relationships with nearby tribals to increase their numbers and then deliver swift retribution.

'I am in grievance of my niece's passing.' Vayu glanced at Sachi, who stood beside him with downcast eyes. She was here because her husband wasn't. One of them had to take decisions. Danger loomed outside Amravati. 'But we must focus on the problem at hand. I heard about a local disturbance close to a village, just a thousand paces from the city.'

'What?' Brihaspati asked.

Vayu had ridden out on his stallion that morning, leaving behind the mist and glory of the city. A dozen soldiers had followed him, all of them armed to the teeth. As chief, he wanted to see for himself the horror and destruction his men had described to him.

A short ride later, he reached a plundered village. Some of his soldiers had been paraded, flogged and beaten, others had been killed.

'What is the meaning of this?' he asked the soldier on his side.

'Narasimha's army is fast approaching Amravati, my lord. Just a few days more and they will come here, to us. The only thing stopping them are our barricades, which are as tall as the skies. Getting past them will be tough.'

Unless one has Vajra. Nara could easily break through the barricades with a bolt from the skies.

Vayu shook his head. 'How many villages?'

'Enough to stop counting, my lord.' The soldier paused with a shudder. 'We need to start building our artillery.'

'Should we attack?' Another soldier brought his mare up from the back, a spear clutched in his free hand.

Vayu contemplated. His sharp eyes were drawn towards the sky, the dew and the mayhem.

'If we remain complacent, we will fade into oblivion, my lord,' the soldier said. 'I say we take them out. All of them. We should send squads and kill each person who dares to come close to us.'

'They will not stop.' Vayu shook his head. 'Retreat. Everyone, retreat!'

'I should have expected this.'

Vayu heard the mutter. He turned around and demanded, 'Who said that?'

No one responded, but Vayu knew. He looked at the soldier he suspected and clenched his fist around his throat, choking him and making his heart beat faster, till he fell to the ground. Vayu looked around sternly, the orange flames of the village reflected in his light irises.

He rode back to Amravati.

'After the incident, I sent emissaries to our other satraps across the country. We are not doing well. Most of our commanders have been assassinated and their lands have been given to Kashyapuri. We are losing revenue. We are losing supplies. We are losing respect with every passing day,' Vayu began.

Sachi and Brihaspati were quiet.

Vayu grunted and ran his fingers through his hair. 'I believe silence is the best option according to you.'

Brihaspati growled. 'Indra doesn't plan to retaliate.'

'That would be wise,' Sachi said, standing up for her husband. 'Especially after what happened the last time he chose to fight back.'

'But we need to do something. Attack. Plan. I don't know.'

'He sits in his room and looks out of the window. Sometimes he walks to Jayanti's room and stays there,' Sachi added, shaking her head.

'Then we must talk,' Vayu said. 'Who do you think he will listen to?'

Sachi and Indra looked at Brihaspati. The old man had been Indra's tutor since the beginning. While Kashyapa was his father, it was Brihaspati who had guided him all along. His bald head, big eyes and wrinkled face, along with the white gown, shone in brilliance at his name.

Brihaspati, the wisest of the sages at Amravati, was respected by everyone. He was considered to be the man behind the Devas' victory in every war. But he was old now and no longer had the zeal with which he used to guide others. There were rumours that his memory was failing, that he was forgetting conversations and even the books he used to read.

'Fine,' Brihaspati said, 'I'll talk to him.'

Indra had been sitting in the balcony, looking at the sunset and the beautiful, opulent city of Amravati that was bathed in shades of grey, white and blue. He was in one of the tall towers, the tallest of which belonged to the king. There were people on the streets, right now looking at the orbs and huge barricades that circled the city. It looked like they were embracing the city, like the embrace of his old man.

He had not spoken much in the last few days. His throat felt parched and he felt a strange numbness. He knew that people thought he was sad. But what Indra felt was nothingness, as if he was a person with no agenda. With no purpose. Most of all, he seemed to have no road to walk on. What was his direction? Where should he go? He had no idea.

He was lost, a broken man with a lost soul. What a tragedy he was, he thought, almost hating himself for what he had become.

'How are you doing, my lord?'

Indra raised his eyebrows and looked up. Brihaspati. He scuttled over with his large shawl, his egg-like body and head bobbing. He sat opposite Indra, on a chair made of oak.

'Fine,' Indra said softly.

'I believe you are not ready to work on the war plans.'

'I don't want to talk about this.'

'I know, and I'm not here because of that.' Brihaspati shook his head. 'I'm here because I remember how you, when you wielded Vajra, were a different man. And now you are a different person. People say power corrupts absolutely. Even good people, moral people.'

'Like Narasimha?'

'Yes. Power is getting to him.'

Indra clenched his jaw. 'Perhaps Rudra was right. He is going to end the world.'

'Do you hate him?'

'I don't know what I feel for him.'

'Vajra, your prized possession, is with him. He's practically undefeatable now. It scares me to think how many people he will kill to reach you.' Brihaspati sighed. 'I remember the day that you had fashioned the Vajra through Tvastr and belittled him for that. He had helped you channelize the power of thunder. But once you had learnt how to do it, you had spewed him out. I remember that man who had to face the brunt when Tvastr created Vritra to kill you.'

Indra arched his brows. *Where is the old man going with this?*

'Jayanti always had a knack for writing. She was a historian of sorts, a little historian.' The old man chuckled. 'She would write all kinds of gibberish. She would read about legends and myths, about heroes and villains. And she would write about them. She would take the quill and let her imagination flow.' Here, Brihaspati frowned. 'I have not told you this, but she had penned down stories about the wars that we lost because we didn't have Vajra. She wrote fantasy tales about you having the Vajra and winning all those fights. Oh, it was something! You know, she wanted to live in a fantasy world because she felt guilty.'

Brihaspati continued, 'I remember telling Jayanti this story. Remember how, to defeat one of the sages from the Asura bloodline, you sent her to distract him. She was your soldier. She was young and feisty, but she was ready. She presented herself as a defector to the sage and told him that she wanted to serve him while you attacked him from behind and destroyed the castle. When she returned, she told you that the sage had told her there was another way for Indra to get his powers back, a simpler way. There was a sage who lived in Illavarti, whose bones Kashyapa had used to create the Devas, to give them powers. This sage was called Dadichi. She asked me if we could find this sage and help you, her father, become powerful again. That was when I told her that she was the Vajra. That he had to let go of his powers to save you.'

'It was you,' Indra breathed, 'who told her.'

'Yes.' He nodded. 'It was better than believing what that Asura sage had told her.'

'But what if she was right? What if there is a way?' Indra leaned forward. 'Jayanti always felt guilty for letting her life be the reason why I had to let go of my powers. What if there are these bones that will allow me to fulfil my daughter's wishes? One last time.'

'Is it about her, or is it about getting power?'

Indra shook his head. 'I don't care about the power. I don't even care about fighting back. But I wonder what Narasimha will do to the people who are close to me. I am not fighting for ambition anymore. I'm fighting for the right thing.'

A fire had been ignited within Indra again. He could feel it. He felt alive. His eyes sparkled.

'Then that must be done.' Brihaspati smiled. 'But what if it's a fool's errand?'

'Then I'm a fool.' Indra smiled.

Indra knew that he had probably never done the right thing for his daughter. He now wished to right this wrong. He planned to do something that would have made her happy, hoping it would give her solace that her death had not been meaningless. That she had succeeded in giving him the push to reclaim the Vajra. So be it, if possible. Indra knew what he had to do.

Not for greed. Not for power. Not for revenge.

He would kill Narasimha.

CHAPTER SEVENTEEN

Parvati remembered the day she had fallen in love. She remembered how safe she had felt in that moment. They had done a job for him—getting a few Mlecchas to scurry, out in the frontiers.

Wearing thick animal fur, they had come to accept the reward. Parvati, as the leader of sorts, had entered the room, in which a bearded man was sitting. He was talking to someone who left when she entered.

'Oh, I believe you have done the job,' he said. 'I'm Bhairav, the one who commissioned you.'

Parvati looked on sternly.

'I didn't speak to you. It was Brahmani, wasn't it?' He had a charming smile.

'Yes. Please give me the coins so I can leave.'

'Well, hold on there. Has anyone told you that you are quite pretty?'

Parvati blushed. She had never been called that. Maybe it was because she barely talked to people outside of her group. 'I … uh … I would like the coins.'

Bhairav looked at her with a searing gaze and a charming smile. He turned and grabbed a pouch of coins, which he tossed at her. 'Here. Now can we speak?'

'What about?'

'You. Yourself. Your interests. Your life. Do you have time?'

Parvati narrowed her gaze. She was not interested in idle conversations with a man, but he was so charming. In any case, the horses were feeding and the rest of her group was busy sharpening their weapons. She decided to stop, not for very long though.

'Sure. We can.'

And the rest, as they say, was history.

He was history.

Tied up against a tree, her arms behind her, Parvati was feeling suffocated. She had been there for as long as she could remember. She had been fed a lot. All sorts of meat and curd and what not. The Vaitarli were fattening her up. The rest of the Matrikas were given the same treatment.

Of course, the Vaitarli wouldn't just kill and eat them. Parvati would see Swapan often, licking his cracked lips. He enjoyed the terror it caused. If Parvati spat out the food, the Vaitarli would torture one of the Matrikas until she ate. They did the same with Parvati when the other Matrikas refused to eat.

One day, he came. He simply looked at her and left. She had a faint memory, but then she was sluggish with sleep.

She couldn't stop crying. She hated herself, her life, the monstrous creature she had birthed. She was furious that she hadn't let Narasimha kill him when there was a chance. She had always believed that good would overpower evil, but Andhaka was beyond evil. He had to be killed.

Parvati's eyes felt heavy. She continued crying, her tears refusing to dry, until she lost consciousness.

When Parvati regained consciousness, her vision was blurred. Her eyes felt like they were weighed down with stones. Her legs and arms were numb, her insides were burning. She wanted to throw up, but there was nothing inside her that could come out. She seemed to be heading straight towards death.

And then she saw him again. A red scarf covered his eyes and bald head. He was smiling menacingly, a black gown enveloping him.

'I thought they would kill you,' he said in a raspy voice. 'But I was wrong. They didn't do it. They haven't eaten in a while and are now preparing a feast. Once they eat, they will regain their powers, and then they will continue to serve me.'

Parvati spat on him. 'I am going to kill you when I get away from here.'

'If you do, mother, if you leave.' He smiled. A cold smile. 'I should let them kill you, but I like this.'

'Why are you here?' She growled. 'Why did you come to this place? You hate it. I know you do.'

'Oh, yes, I do. You are right about that. But there's a reason. Wouldn't you like to know?' He grinned. 'I learnt something recently. Something important. I realized that I should delve deeper and find out more. Maybe I will find what I'm looking for. It belonged to my father.'

'You killed your father.'

'Oh, not that sham. My real father—Hiranyaksha.'

'He was your torturer.'

'Well, the more I learn about him, the more I realize that he wanted to toughen me up for the world.'

'Probably, yes. But he hated you. He hated your guts and your bloodline.'

'Indeed. Perfection requires sacrifice.'

'And you think you are perfect?'

'I might be. He left me something. He loved me, I know.' He grinned. 'That's why he left this army for me. I didn't know anything about this until I got his message. It came late, but it came at the right time.'

Parvati looked at Brahmani, Chamundi, Narasimhi and the others tied to the trees, unable to move.

'See you soon.' Andhaka smiled. 'It's good we had this conversation. It's bad that it's our last one.'

With that, he left. Torches blared around the Matrikas. Parvati knew she had to do something. She had been feeling delirious for some time now, but this conversation with Andhaka had awakened something within her. She began to push her bangles towards her wrists, as the Vaitarli chanted at a distance..

I need to escape this place.

She knew she had to break her bangles. The serrated edges would help her cut the rope. But that could also lead to her slashing her veins. Carefully, but quickly, she smashed the bangles against the trunk of the tree. She grabbed the shards and grinned. Some of the shards were causing her pain, but she knew she wasn't seriously injured. With one edge of a broken bangle, she began to cut through the rope.

And then it began to rain. Parvati couldn't see clearly. She cried, continuing to cut into the rope until she felt the grip around her arms loosen. With a smile, she jerked her body forward. She felt an instant stab in the stomach because a branch was stuck in her, but she pulled it away and began to untie her feet.

She fell to the ground when the ropes gave way, scarcely breathing, her fingers sinking into the mud. She couldn't believe she was free. Feeling both triumphant and hopeful, she began to untie the other Matrikas, slapping them to wake them up.

Chamundi almost screamed when she was woken up, but Parvati silenced her. Soon, with all of them untied, the Matrikas began to move.

'We need to be careful.'

Most of them were sluggish, barely able to walk. 'I don't know what I feel,' Brahmani said.

'We need to go after Andhaka.' Parvati directed the group away from the Vaitarli, until …

There was a loud cry. The Matrikas turned around. The Vaitarli had seen them.

It was time to run.

CHAPTER EIGHTEEN

Garuda was missing Sonapatra.

Unwell for a while now, he was confined to his quarters. His stomach didn't feel fine, his body was burning up with fever and his eyes were constantly droopy. But the worst part was that Sonapatra was nowhere to be seen.

Garuda asked his soldiers to call her. To summon her. To find her if they could. But she was gone. She was nowhere. It was as if she was nobody.

Perhaps you have been attacked …

He felt guilty. Everything had gone wrong after Vaashkal's trespassing. He should have known the man was dangerous. Now, even Ayurveda was unable to cure him. Wiping away his tears, he lay in bed clenching his stomach, hoping for things to be all right soon.

He wrote a letter. There were some things Narasimha needed to know, but Garuda barely had the energy to write.

And because this information was for Nara's ears only, he didn't want to summon the scribe to write on his behalf.

Finally, Garuda wrote the letter himself. He understood the importance of sharing such information in person, but a letter was the next best thing. Having finished writing, he placed the letter on one side.

A soldier entered, perturbed. It was a Suparn. 'How are you doing, chief?'

Garuda was sweating. 'I need help. But more than that, I need you to send this to Nara. Make sure it is delivered only to him and no one else.'

The soldier nodded. 'But his guards check everything.'

'Tell him it's from Garuda,' he said and fell back on the bed, waiting for the inevitable.

That was when he heard the voice. The damned voice. 'If it comes from me, there will be no checking.'

Garuda and the soldier turned to see that it was none other than the orange-haired Vaashkal, with his bronze eyes and disarming smile, a long shawl wrapped over a colourful gown.

'Oh, I'm sorry, but they let me in. They said you were ill.'

'Lord Vaashkal, how are you doing?' The soldier bowed.

'Much better. But your leader seems to be quite ill.' He had a mischievous smile about him. 'I think one of the soldiers was calling you. I'll take the letter.'

Garuda wanted to protest, but Vaashkal grabbed it from the soldier's hand, who closed the door as he left the room. Garuda wanted to speak, but he was in too much agony.

'Oh well, you have been a naughty boy.' Vaashkal smiled, opening the letter. He read it and said, 'Ah, so you know.'

'You are dead. I'll make sure you are dead.'

Vaashkal leaned forward, smiling. 'I believe it is *you* who is poisoned and about to die. Not me.'

Poison?

'Are we sure we are doing the right thing?' Dhriti asked.

Prahlad was pushing against the crowd, wearing a hood. Dhriti, too, was shoving her way ahead, but she did not have the same clarity of purpose that Prahlad did.

'Yes,' Prahlad said.

They were close to the gates of the city. There were soldiers, Asuras, looking at each person who was leaving, checking their identification.

'But why?' Dhriti asked.

'Because I'll face a trial for treason if I stay here.' Prahlad licked his lips in worry. He wasn't able to understand what to do, where to go further, as the guards began to circle and look at him. 'I just learnt that he wanted to summon me, and I cannot risk it. I betrayed him and, based on his state of mind, he will try to kill me.'

'I think you are overthinking this,' Dhriti said. 'I'm sure he will understand.'

'You didn't see him killing the girl with his bare claws. I did. And I know he's not the same person anymore.'

As Prahlad moved ahead, his eyes met those of the soldiers. One of them stood before him almost instantaneously.

'My lord, we ask you to come with us.'

Prahlad stopped. He didn't know what to do. He wanted to punch the guard, maybe even stab him, but that would mean facing a trial for murder, which would mean being hanged to death. Dhriti grabbed his hands and held on tightly.

'Let me go.'

'I believe we cannot,' the guard said. He grabbed Prahlad's arm and began to pull him.

Prahlad pushed the guard away. He turned to look at Dhriti, ready to storm out, when he saw more soldiers crowding around him. He knew he had no choice but to comply. He had his sword on him, and he knew he could use it.

But what was the point?

'Can I sit by your side, my friend?' Vaashkal asked. Though his words sounded like he was asking for permission, he actually wasn't. He smiled as he sat down.

'You poisoned me,' said Garuda.

'Yes, indeed. I did.' Vaashkal said. 'Oh, it's a slow-moving poison. The right amount makes you writhe in pain. It can make you hate yourself. And then you feel this burn inside of you, bringing you to a point where you think killing yourself is better than living.'

'You are not going to get away with it.'

'Get away with what?'

'With whatever you are up to.'

'Oh, you need to realize, you need to be absolutely sure what you are talking about. You have no idea what I am up to.'

'Nara is smart. He sees through you.'

'But he can't get rid of me. I give him victories. I am like a necessary evil in his life, which you or Prahlad could never become. Both of you adhered to morality, while I took the immoral route.'

'How … how'—Garuda coughed—'how did you poison me?'

'The wine. But I must say that it wasn't the same wine that Narasimha drank. He drank a poison of sorts, too, which works to bring out the instinctive side. It makes you let go of rationality.'

'That's why'—Garuda shivered and breathed—'that's why he's doing all of this.'

'Tsk, tsk.' Vaashkal shook his head. 'He's doing this because he wants to. It's instinctive, remember. It brings your heart's desires to the fore. I am just an instrument, an instrument he has the intent to use. It's not my fault.'

'I will find out. I will find out why you are doing this. And then I will kill you.'

Vaashkal grinned. 'I'm helping my king. What are you doing, except being absolutely useless?'

Prahlad was nudged into a room, a long chamber that he had been in often. It was the king's room, the main hall with its tall marble pillars, a red carpet gracing the marble floor and a pedestal on which the iron throne stood. He saw someone in the shadows. The head was bent, but the mane was recognizable. On the mane, where the lion's eyes were—it glimmered.

The man was bare-chested but wearing a golden dhoti. There were no guards or soldiers around.

Prahlad worried for his life. He knew he wasn't as strong as Narasimha; he never could be. But he walked forward with firm steps. Lord Vishnu would save him as always, but Narasimha was an Avatar of Lord Vishnu ...

Who would save him now? Was there anyone beyond the Supreme?

'I was called here.' Prahlad stated a fact.

'Because you were running away,' Narasimha said. 'And I wonder why?' His voice was low, almost threatening but with a heavy, husky grunt to it.

'I was leaving for some personal business. Can I not do so?'

'Does that business have anything to do with taking me down as the king?'

Prahlad had expected this. 'I believe you have been informed.'

'Of course I have.'

'I had my reasons.'

'I'm sure you did.' Nara came out of the shadows, yet his lion-face was visible as he towered next to Prahlad. 'How long has it been since you went to Hiranyapur?'

Prahlad's eyes narrowed. 'It's been quite long. I went last when I was a kid.'

'Good. Then you might remember the way,' Nara said. After a slight pause, he added, 'I don't hate you, kid. In fact, I love you. I know whatever you did was out of the innocence of your heart. You didn't mean any harm.'

Nara put his hands on Prahlad's shoulder, squeezing it as Prahlad's heartbeat began to slow down. 'I want you to go to Hiranyapur. Unfortunately, there has been some disturbance there. Maitali, the preceptress of the Danavs, is taking too long to leave. Now, I wonder why that is happening, because my men are already there, trying to ensure the Danavs leave for the Pataal islands. If you go there and nudge them out, it will help.'

'I don't know if this is even a duty.' Prahlad recognized that Nara's demand was unnecessary and nonsensical. But he understood why Nara was doing this. Sending Prahlad to Hiranyapur would ensure he was kept away, but under watch so that he didn't do anything suspicious.

'It is. An important one.'

Prahlad nodded and bowed slightly. 'Your wish is my command.'

'Good.'

Prahlad had just turned to leave when he heard Nara call out. 'One more thing, Prahlad.'

'Yes?' Prahlad didn't turn. He knew something unpleasant was coming.

'Don't ever try doing what you did again. Don't ever go against me.'

It wasn't a threat, but it sure felt like one to Prahlad.

'So this is it. I'm almost out of the way. You can continue to do whatever you are doing,' Garuda said.

'I give you a day or so,' Vaashkal said with his lips pursed. 'I'm sure it had to end this way.'

Garuda grabbed Vaashkal by the collar. 'You won't get away with this. My curse will haunt you forever. I've told Sonapatra about what you have done. She will ensure everyone knows.'

'You told the girl I sent to you? Oh darling, you need to know who you are making friends with!'

'No …' Garuda's pupils dilated. It was impossible. 'I was saved by the poison earlier, I can have soma …'

'There's no soma here … you can't get it.'

Garuda tried to find the bell and ring it, but Vaashkal threw it out of the window.

'Rot and suffer, Garuda.' Vaashkal smiled.

Garuda saw him leaving the room. The last thing he said was: 'Narasimha will know. He will know who you are.'

'Who am I?' Vaashkal asked.

Garuda closed his eyes, but not before muttering the last thing he had read in the letter Hiranyakashyap had addressed to Vaashkal: 'Prahlad's brother, the scion to the throne of Kashyapuri.'

CHAPTER NINETEEN

Indra prepared for the voyage.

Now, some people might say it was a fool's errand while others might think it was the right thing to do. Indra himself had no idea; he didn't even care any more. He knew there would always be naysayers, and those naysayers were …

Vayu stood on the porch and looked at the caravans that were being prepared. The horses had been fed, the food had been stocked and the elephants had been called. The docks had been informed and the ships were ready. Lord Indra was leaving with most of his army, leaving Amravati vulnerable to an attack from Narasimha.

Brihaspati came up to Vayu. 'You seem perturbed.'

'What is he doing?'

'Fulfilling his daughter's wishes.'

'You did this, old man,' Vayu rasped. 'You should know that this is not the time to go on a stupid mission. He's failing his country and his people. We are at war, but we are going to retrieve the bones of a dead sage! Am I the only one who thinks this is ridiculous? My brother is leading us straight into the ashes.'

Brihaspati nodded. 'Why don't you tell him? As far as I know, we are going with him.'

'Well, he's the king, so we have to obey.' Vayu growled, regretting that he wasn't one. 'The ocean makes me sick. Varuna always made fun of me for that when we were children.' He shook his head.

'Indra needs you. Sometimes the winds may not be favourable. You have to ensure the winds help them get there faster.'

'Yeah, I'm his guide. That's what I've become.' Vayu shrugged and turned to leave to ensure all his food, clothes and supplies were packed. 'Do we even know where we are going? Where are these bones?'

Indeed, Indra knew. He hadn't told Brihaspati or Vayu because the way he had found out about the location had been shocking. He didn't want them to worry.

After his conversation with Brihaspati, Indra had scrounged through his daughter's room for her books and journals. He was exhausted after shifting beds, searching cupboards and even breaking walls. Before long, the room was in disarray and Indra was standing in a corner gasping. Just as he lay down, he heard footsteps.

'What on earth have you done to our daughter's room?' Sachi asked.

'I'm searching for the truth,' Indra said. 'You wouldn't understand.'

Sachi, with her face hovering over Indra, said, 'You don't think I will understand? I can't see you going down like this.'

'I'm doing what is right for our daughter.'

'And I am not? You have a kingdom to protect. You can't just ... you can't just become what you are becoming.'

'I know. But if I get the bones, I'll be able to get my powers back. I am a weak old man without my powers and Narasimha ... well, he's stronger than me. I need to find ...' Indra paused, choking up. 'I cannot believe I let our sweet little cherub go to the Asuras to distract them. She was ... she would have been so scared. Oh dear, what a sick, twisted father I am!'

'She went by choice. She wanted to help you, and she was not young. She was far more mature than you could ever hope to be.'

Indra was still sprawled on the floor, unable to get up. He felt heavy, as if his daughter was glaring at him in disappointment from the afterlife. 'I am looking for something she had written about Dadichi's bones. It is impossible ...' Indra paused abruptly.

'What happened?'

Indra's eyes were focused on the journal that he had just spotted under the bed. He dragged it out and began to flip through the pages hurriedly. He found an entry from the last few days of his daughter's life at the Asura's lair, when she had been swaying a coconut leaf over the sage's head to pamper him.

I did not the know the sage's name, neither did I care. But the peace on his face was admirable. He was a beautiful man, a man of chastity. He would care for me and give me treats. He would treat me like a lover, and I had no idea why. I was too young for him, but he didn't mind. He would never touch me inappropriately, and he would always respect me. In fact, all the Asuras did.

I came here as a maid, but they treated me like one of their own. I wonder why. Was my father wrong in telling me how vicious these brutes were? Because they didn't seem like that at all.

But the sage, he was wise and had travelled far and wide. I knew he would have the answer to a question I was afraid of asking the people back home.

'Where do the Devas get their powers?' I ventured.

The sage looked at me and smiled. 'Oh, aren't you a curious one?'

'I always wondered, my lord, and I hope my curiosity is not a problem.'

'Not at all. I love inquisitive people.' The sage continued, 'Kashyapa, the father of the Devas and Asuras, decided he wanted to bestow the Devas with power, so that they would have an upper hand over the Asuras. He went to Dadichi, one of the wisest sages who ever lived. Kashyapa performed the yagna there, finally conquering true power, which he gave to the Devas.'

'I see. But what about Tvastr?'

'Oh, that's another myth. Some say that Tvastr had fashioned these powers from the elements of the earth to give to Kashyapa.'

'But which version is true?'

'The Dadichi version. Where do you think Tvastr got the elements from? From the bones of Dadichi, of course. The sage *had sacrificed himself so that Tvastr could use the elements and give Kashyapa the power he desired. But, for the sacrifice, Kashyapa had to perform the yagna I mentioned earlier.'*

'Ah, interesting. Have all the bones been used?'

'Some say they have. Others say there are still some bones that, if used, can give the Devas more power than they could ever hope for. The Asuras have tried to find these bones. Well, I guess I should be honest.' The sage shrugged. 'I know they are in the great, deep ocean.'

I listened carefully because these were some very important details, which I have sketched below. I am quite certain about the location the sage was indicating. But I wasn't sure how correct it was. I knew I had to speak to Brihaspati and confide in him, though it would be considered stupid. The sage was talking of a myth, a myth in which he had not found the bones. In fact, he had supposedly met the serpent, which had been huge and scary. The Asuras broke lot of ships and destroyed most of their supplies. They returned after losing several men. The sage had called it 'false hope'. Probably the bones might be in the serpent's stomach.

But the sage could be wrong.

It is possible that the bones were never there. In any case, such a voyage sounds too risky, and I don't want Father to be distracted. Perhaps I'll tell him some day.

After all, I have all the time in the world to inform him about this.

The last line hit Indra hard. It made him want to cry. His daughter's journal didn't mention why there was a serpent in the first place. Dadichi had probably been swallowed by one as a sacrifice. But Indra held a map in his hands. It was haphazardly drawn and depicted an area east of Amaravati—out in the sea. Indra grinned.

'I found it. I found it!' he yelled and jumped up, his bones hurting. He embraced his wife, ignoring her sharp words from moments ago. 'I FOUND IT!'

'What is going on? What have you found?'

'We are going on a journey,' he said, caressing her cheeks. 'A journey that our daughter wanted us to go on.'

On his way to the docks, Indra thought about the day he had found the journal.

It had been a while. Days had gone by as the procession passed through meadows and wastelands, carrying oxen and cows. Thousands of soldiers were accompanying him. Indra would switch between his elephant, his mare and the caravan, depending on how bored and exhausted he was.

The docks were still far. The procession had already encountered some robbers and marauders who had been handed punishments.

Indra ordered a feast to mark the momentous journey.

'My dear friends,' he said, addressing everyone amidst the sound of trumpets and flutes, 'thank you for supporting me. Believe me when I say that this journey will be a milestone in all our lives. We are going to find the mythical bones of Dadichi, the very sage my father had bowed to. Don't do this for me, but do it for my father. It's because of him that we are all here.'

He looked at the concerned faces of Vayu, Sachi and Brihaspati, who remained quiet. He smiled and decided to

ignore them. *When they see me all-powerful again, they'll
know ... they'll know I was right.*

During the feast, Indra left to read his daughter's journal
in solace. Reading it felt like hearing his daughter's voice
in his head. He noticed that the lights in his tent had been
dimmed. He wondered why and entered—there was a man,
and a rope ...

A shadow grabbed his throat and pinned him down.

Indra began to choke. He was shocked, but he struggled
and managed to stand up, pushing the shadow down to the
ground. He turned around to see that his own guard had
attacked him.

How dare he ...

The soldier, however, didn't give up. He hit Indra on the
sole, making him kneel in pain, and punched him hard on the
face. Indra fell, blood spewing from his mouth.

'I should have just stabbed you, old man!' The soldier
brought down a knife, aiming for Indra's heart. But Indra
pulled the journal in front of him. The knife pierced the
hardbound.

Pushing the journal towards the soldier, Indra knocked
him down. He pulled the knife away and noticed that his
assassin was bleeding. He grabbed the soldier by the throat
and brought the knife close to his neck.

'Who sent you?'

'You can't trust anyone. The people closest to you want you
dead.'

Indra growled. 'Do not speak to me in riddles. Tell me
clearly. Who is it?'

'My family will be killed,' the soldier cried, 'if I say anything.'

'Tell me, or you will be tortured.'

'My son has been promised a thousand coins. I'm sorry, old man,' the soldier said and then brought his neck close to the knife and slashed it. Seconds later, he was dead.

Indra pulled back, horrified.

And betrayed.

Closest to me ...

I can't trust anyone.

CHAPTER TWENTY

Parvati had forgotten how long she had been running for.

It was the dead of night, but the Vaitarli were still chasing. She had made the crossing, zigzagging and jumping as she passed coves and steep cliffs, letting the snow seep into her. She could see Brahmani, Chamundi and Narasimhi keeping up with her.

'They have taken our weapons!' Brahmani exclaimed.

Parvati turned her head. The torches were still blazing. She could hear them humming and chanting. The Vaitarli were chasing them with stones and sticks and …

'Using our weapons against us,' she said, struggling to breathe. 'We need to get rid of them. Kill them, if we must.'

'There are hundreds of them,' Brahmani said. 'How do you plan to kill hundreds?'

Parvati had no answer. She was fighting fatigue and her body was threatening to give up. She could feel her bones hurting. Every movement amplified the pain in her wounds and bruises.

'We have no choice but to get away,' she said finally.

She could see the land of Hiranyapur. There were no animals around, except vultures that were waiting for them to drop dead. There were desolate villages and broken caverns. Death was all around. Beyond a cliff, on the barren snowy land, Parvati saw a castle of sorts. Ravens were circling it. It jutted out as an oddity, with towers that stood tall and firm. It felt deserted.

'There's a cliff. We need to jump,' Parvati said.

'And kill ourselves?' Brahmani asked.

'There's a stream. If we position ourselves right … we will be fine.'

Brahmani didn't like the idea, but she hadn't been in charge for a while now. Parvati had taken over.

She made it past the cliff, an arrow flew past her and pierced Chamundi's shoulder. The dark-skinned woman pulled the arrow out and, with venomous eyes, watched the immortal beings move towards her.

'If we had the weapons, we could have killed them. Why waste energy on those who can't even die?' Parvati said, looking over the cliff, fifty feet down, at the stream that zigzagged towards the castle.

'It'll be freezing. If we are lucky enough to not have our heads crack open down there, we might freeze to death,' said Narasimhi.

'Probably. But we can get out as soon as we enter,' said Parvati, sighting a stony pathway close to the stream that they could use.

'Fine! Fine!' Brahmani grimaced. 'Let's just do it. I hope you are right about this, Parvati.'

Parvati wasn't sure. The stream was wide and large.

Forget it. I'll do it.

Parvati was the first one to jump. As a gush of wind pushed her down, she felt her heart make its way out of her chest. Her mouth felt parched and her face lost colour.

As her body splashed into the stream, the water engulfed her and a chill seeped into her bruises. She gasped for breath as she tried to make it to the surface, trying to find her way to the shore. She heard the others fall into the water behind her.

Once she got to the shore, she realized that most of them were safe. They couldn't hear the hums and chants anymore. Taking deep breaths, they sighed and tried to rest.

As they dried themselves, Brahmani said, 'We did it. I am thankful to the gods of water.'

Parvati grinned. She felt a certain sense of responsibility towards this group. She was glad they had escaped the Vaitarli. They began making their way down the stony path.

'Now what?' Brahmani asked.

Parvati looked at the castle. It was right there, at the end of the stream, standing tall, a beacon among the rocks and stones.

'We face Andhaka.'

Parvati's thoughts went towards him. As the Matrikas moved forward, her mind went back to the time when Bhairav and she had been trying to have a child. She had hoped for a settled life after marriage, but it had seemed impossible given that she was a part of the Matrikas who first worked for Indra and later alone. But Bhairav had promised her a normal married life.

She remembered sitting in a corner of her home, observing the daily goings-on at Shiva's fort. Something or the other always kept happening. There were no dull moments.

'Are you still thinking about it?' A voice had beckoned as she had sat in her house. Parvati had turned to see her bearded husband smile at her and let out a husky laugh. 'Do not worry, my love,' he had said and sat next to her. 'Everything will be fine,' he had added and placed his hands over her head.

'Easy for you to say.' Parvati had shaken her head. 'I haven't told you something.'

'And that is?'

'I was cursed a long time back, as a child, by a guru.'

'A guru?' Her husband had raised his brows.

'I know they are not allowed to teach women, but he did. He was different,' she had said. 'And I was just an orphan girl whom he broke. So, he cursed me.'

'What was the curse?'

'That I would end up hurting the people I love and that I wouldn't live a happy life.'

'Well, I hope you prove him wrong. Because we will live a happy life for sure.' He had smiled. 'Forever and ever and ever.'

Parvati had clenched her jaw in response. The curse had felt real to her. She had sensed that things weren't in their favour even though there was love between them.

'I think I should visit him,' she had said.

'Is he alive?'

'I do not know. I can beg for his forgiveness.' Parvati had arched her brows. 'What do you think?'

'Do what makes you feel secure. Do what makes you feel safe,' he had said. 'I'll come with you.'

'You have too much to do here. I will go. At least that way I will know that I tried everything.'

Bhairav had nodded and kissed Parvati. The next week, Parvati and her band of guards had made the trip to the Gurukul. Parvati hadn't been sure if she was doing the right thing. When they finally reached the guru's abode, after crossing lands, after the sun had come closer than it should have and scorched the earth, they found that the Gurukul had been destroyed. No one lived there. It was deserted. The place where she had spent a lot of her childhood was a thing of the past.

She had realized that she could either cling to the past or let it change her. She had returned to her husband and, a month later, learnt that she was pregnant.

Maybe the curse was not effective. Maybe it was not real. Maybe …

Parvati was wrong.

It was real, very real. She escaped the thoughts flooding her mind and focused on the castle. This was one of the few castles where all she saw was creepers and vines, and branches of trees forming zigzag shapes on the stony hedges of the building. There were no people and no guards, just wolves watching them from a distance. By the time the Matrikas got to the castle, they had armed themselves with branches, just in case there was a sudden attack.

The castle was so desolate and so silent that Parvati felt as if she was stepping into another world.

The castle had belonged to Hiranyaksha when he had been stationed here. This was where he had kept his secrets. This was the reason why Andhaka, who hated his stepfather so much that he had killed his real father for it, found redemption by learning secrets.

What did Andhaka learn? Parvati was curious.

Through the silence, mist and fog, Parvati and Brahmani entered the castle.

'Scout the area,' Parvati said to the remaining Matrikas. 'Alert us if you find anyone.'

Brahmani walked into all the rooms inside, opening the doors with caution. 'Do you think he's here?'

'Had he been here, he would have showed himself. This means he has left.'

'Then why are we here? We should chase him.'

'We will investigate. We need to know why he was here,' Parvati said. And then she noticed a path that went down to a narrow galley, into a basement.

She moved downstairs with Brahmani. Thanks to her wet clothes, she was sneezing and coughing, and her nose was blocked. But the secret surrounding the castle and Andhaka's presence there haunted her. She wondered why he had been there, when had he left, and why.

The basement, she noticed, was a lair. There were tables and chairs and the room smelled of a lot of dead things. She looked at the papers, folders and papyrus spread out.

'Just have a look,' she said to Brahmani.

She went through the pages, reading all of them. Many of them outlined Hiranyaksha's expansion plans. They included his personal journals, his idea to create a sky bridge between Pataal and Illavarti and what not. One of the papers mentioned his will. Many papers were torn, until ...

She saw letters. Addressed to many people. One of them was addressed to someone he called his child.

Child ... must be Andhaka.

She began to skim through it.

Dear child,

I believe your journey has been fruitful. You have come a long way for me. I had instructed the Vaitarli to deliver the message to you on a particular name day. Hoping that I would deliver what I took from you a long time ago. I made you weak. I made you worse.

All I wanted was for you to be strong. I wanted you to grow. I wanted you to face all kinds of misery before learning that this world is good to tough men. Only the tough men rule. No one else.

I must give you some context about why I mistreated you, why I treated you like a slave.

A long time ago, as I journeyed to all parts of the country, after my migration, I realized what a bad place this was: full of misery, hopelessness, darkness, violence and what not. I was disappointed, but I travelled nonetheless. I chanced upon a Gurukul where I met a guru who was old and weak. His memory was giving him trouble, but he told me a lot about the

Matrikas and Skanda, the prophetic hero of this land. I was enamoured by these myths. As I was preparing to leave, I realized that these myths were too precious to be shared with anyone else.

I knew I had to save the world. I had to find Skanda. And so I burnt the Gurukul down and killed the man who spoke to me.

I forgot about the myths as I continued to work at Yakshlok. I then opened up this land so I could rule from the north while my brother established himself in the south.

That was until I met you. I was fascinated that you were born out of a Matrika and that you would grow to be a Skanda. I was delighted! Through you, I could finally right the wrong in this country and make it better. I could help it grow.

But as you matured, I saw that you were weak. You were always sick. You wanted a woman to take care of you. That was not the kind of hero I had envisioned you to be. This was why I began to hurt you. I began to destroy you from within. I began preparing you for what the world could do to you, but I was training you. I blinded you so that your other senses could become stronger. I broke your soul because then you would realize how the brain is far superior to your sword.

And now I'm giving it all back to you. Lead the army I am leaving behind. They are immortals. They will live for long after I am gone. Lead them to victory.

I am also leaving a potion—a potion of soma and some herbs that you may not be familiar with, but it is *potent. Your eyes will be healed. You will be powerful. This potion will give you strength you have never imagined. And you deserve it. You should have it.*

Why, you may ask. What is your purpose, you may wonder.

I realized when I was on my deathbed that the country we live in doesn't deserve the Devas or the Asuras. It deserves a hero. You should start with taking control of whatever my brother has. He is not as astute as the others. From there, keep expanding.

So that is it. Be my Skanda.

Parvati read the letter again. It sounded like a fanatic raging. Someone had taken a myth so seriously that it had destroyed someone's life.

She couldn't believe it.

'What is it?' Brahmani asked, her voice echoing.

'Andhaka can see,' Parvati said. 'And I know where he is going to start his campaign.'

Kashyapuri.

'We need to leave.'

'Yes, this place is smelling, too,' Brahmani remarked.

But why was it smelling?

Parvati looked around, trying to see through the shadows and darkness. As she moved into the corners, she saw that the room was full of corpses lined up in corners. And all of them looked like Andhaka. They had been slaughtered. Parvati was horrified.

He murdered them all!

'What is the meaning of this?' Brahmani asked. She, too, had noticed the corpses.

'It means we are in big trouble,' Parvati said. 'He has killed his duplicates … because he doesn't need them any more.'

One of the corpses, she noticed, had had his eyes gouged out.

CHAPTER TWENTY-ONE

Prahlad had been trekking towards Hiranyapur—the land of the giants—with Dhriti by his side and a dozen of Narasimha's soldiers.

As a child, he had heard stories from his father. Stories about the large men who lived in Hiranyapur—the Danavs. The city had been designed for them, with houses and other buildings ten times bigger than ordinary. Larger than usual rivers had been carved out, and the skies were different. Located in the dusty plains, east of Yakshlok, Hiranyapur offered enough space to the Danavs. There was something strange about the place. Prahlad was not sure whether the stories were true or not.

But as he grew up, he realized it was no fantasy land after his father took him to meet his Aunt Maitali, who was then the leader of the Danavs.

Now, the Danavs didn't speak much, but they could be idiosyncratic. If you gave them orders, they would obey. But if you didn't, they would simply eat and sleep. And they were giants, of course. But Maitali was different. She was intelligent and, though not fifty feet tall like the others, she was over eight feet tall with long legs and a strong spine.

The travel to Hiranyapur was tough, especially during the journey through the dusty plains of Yakshlok. They had to endure a lot of dust and storms of sand and locate oases for water to drink. Though they were travelling with mares and camels, they stopped to catch their breath often. Not once did Prahlad tell Dhriti what he was feeling. He was worried somebody would hear and misinterpret his words. Even a single word against the crown could lead to his beheading.

He often cried at night. He felt like a prisoner, even though he wasn't. He had roused the council and found people who had supported him, only for the majority to ultimately go against him.

During this long journey, he had found a guard—a special guard who was loyal to Lord Narasimha—named Shantaram. He was a quiet man with a scar on his cheek and a dagger hanging across his chest, shielded with a special scabbard.

One night, Shantaram said to Prahlad, 'My lord, it is great that you are going there.'

A bonfire burned close to them to fight the intense cold. Only Shantaram and Prahlad were awake.

'There's been a lot of disturbance in the city as it is. Stay away from danger.' Shantaram. sounded concerned.

'You saying that makes me even more concerned. Aren't you here to kill me if I do something wrong?'

'Oh, that's my duty, but you are a good man. However, remember that my duty is more important to me than morality,' Shantaram said with a cheeky grin, displaying his two missing teeth. 'Lord Vaashkal is my employer, and if it wasn't for King Narasimha I would have assassinated you. The king really cares about you. I used to be part of your father's army, but I wasn't treated well. Lord Vaashkal has been kind. He ensured my family didn't starve. He gave me land, he gave me crops to grow. He is my god. Now I don't know what the others would say or feel about this, even you, but I owe him everything.'

Prahlad raised his eyebrows. He had never heard about this side of Vaashkal—about how he had amassed so much wealth and followers. *If he has attained this level, he must have done something right.* 'Your employer sounds like a good man,' Prahlad managed to say.

But for me, he is the enemy.

By the time they reached Hiranyapur, Prahlad was exhausted. He felt the journey would kill him, and if that was Vaashkal's plan, then so be it.

He was on his horse with Dhriti behind him. 'How are you holding up?' she asked.

'I do not know.'

'Well, how does it feel to be here?'

Prahlad knew what she was talking about. In front of him were desolate lands, tall towers and castles and the giants. He had seen them from a distance. They were so huge that they seemed to be touching the sky. Prahlad could see that they were busy preparing the longships for the great ocean that was not very far. There were caravans and a lot of horses. Each time a Danav moved, the ground trembled.

'They look scary.'

'They won't hurt us.'

'How do you know?'

'Because they only attack those who threaten them, and no one *dares* to threaten them.'

Prahlad rode forward, his entourage following him.

'How come they just agreed to leave?' Dhriti asked.

'Because they didn't want to be involved in politics or any unnecessary bloodshed. Danavs, despite their size, are simple people. You give them a home and ten buffaloes to eat and they will be good to go.'

'Sounds simple enough,' she said sarcastically.

Prahlad rode faster as the gates of Hiranyapur were opened to him. The guards there had a simple job, stationed by Narasimha only when they were leaving. They were there to make sure Maitali left with the Danavs.

While Dhriti rested, Prahlad walked around with Shantaram.

They had entered the tall halls, which were over a hundred feet in height, escorted by women twice their size to the dinner table where Maitali waited for them.

Prahlad was wearing a girdle and long kurta that was glimmering with gold, rings and pointed sandal. Though Maitali was his father's cousin, his second cousin to be precise, and Prahlad wasn't directly related to her, he still called her his aunt.

The dinner table was a lot longer than what they had anticipated. Prahlad, surprised at the quantity of food laid out, saw the mead and wine that had been poured out for them. And then Prahlad saw the tall woman.

Maitali.

A beautiful woman, she bent down with a smile and hugged him. She had big bronze eyes and an infectious smile. Prahlad saw Shantaram standing in the corner with the other guards.

'I'm sorry, nephew, about the food. I would have cooked more, but most of the hands are busy in preparing the ships. We are leaving in the next few weeks.' She smiled and sat on one end of the long table. Prahlad took a sip of the mead that was handed to him.

'One might wonder why you are here?' Maitali asked.

'One should be happy that I'm here. I wanted to bid farewell.' Prahlad smiled.

Maitali didn't respond with the same warmth. 'Pardon my suspicion, but you have been accused of regicide. You killed your father, my cousin.'

'I assisted in killing him,' Prahlad said. 'He was bringing about our downfall.'

'Hiranyaksha suspected that. He was smarter than your father, I should tell you.' She drank from her goblet. 'I am not surprised you had to put him down. The last time I met him, he did seem like he was losing it. The armour and the blade, they had got to him.'

Prahlad nodded. 'Yes. Power corrupts.' It was true; it had been proved time and again. 'Aunty, I come here with pure intentions. To bid farewell to you and to see you off. I have no reason to make insidious plots against you. I am but a humble boy.'

'Who is getting his facial hair. Quite charming,' she said with a laugh. 'But tell me, are you here because our departure is delayed? Kashyapuri will be churning with gossip about why we have not left yet. I could erase their suspicions by blaming the delay on a glitch, but then I enjoy giving them a little trouble.'

Prahlad grinned as he sliced through the roast placed before him. 'I'm sure, Aunty. How are the giants doing?'

'Pretty sad after everything your father did. They are disappointed in him, and in you too. It was their decision to leave actually. I wanted to conquer more, but they asked me what the point was. They want to live peacefully.'

Prahlad nodded. 'It is best for everyone.'

'Do you honestly believe that the current ruler is the right man? Don't you think your father was better?' Maitali was curious.

Prahlad glanced at Shantaram, who was quiet. 'Lord Narasimha is my king, the only true king.'

'I wonder what they have done to you. Have they brainwashed you?' Maitali frowned.

Prahlad could sense Maitali was not happy. She wanted a little nudge, a little convincing.

'Is the conniving Vaashkal behind this? I'm sure he is.' She shook her head and grunted. 'He has spoiled everything. I may not know him well, but I do know that his mother died early and that his father was a reckless drunk. Vaashkal apparently grew tired of him and was accused of killing him. I remember he had come here with Hiranyakashyap once. By then, he was already an executive in the treasury. Of course, this was before he gained strong allies and grew in stature. He really has a footprint now.'

'Yes. He's a clever man.'

'Those are the ones my nan warned me to stay away from. We are done now. All we want is to go home and reclaim Pataal. This crusade of coming all the way here was stupidity, all because of your father and uncle.'

Prahlad nodded. As he ate, he saw someone entering the room. He came to Maitali to have her sign some papers. He was clearly not an Asura, Danav or Deva. He was a Manav. He was clumsy and short, shorter than Prahlad, who had shot up in height in the last couple of days.

Once they finished their work, Maitali said, 'Oh, where are my manners? Meet the smartest man I've ever met, the man who holds all the knowledge and information pertaining to this country. He is well travelled and writes poems. Also, he is going to Pataal with me, to learn about the Asuras. Quite a charming man, I must say! His name is Narayana.' She then turned to Narayana and said, 'This is my nephew, Prahlad.'

Narayana came forward to greet Prahlad, who remained seated and simply nodded before going back to eating his food. Narayana left the room shortly after that.

'Why did you ask me whether he's the right king or not?' Prahlad asked.

'I've heard rumours that he's causing mayhem. I have my ravens there, you know, squawking to me the smallest of details. I wanted to trouble him and enter, even spread the rumour that I would come, but we are just not motivated enough to. Also, the last time I offered to help your father, he rejected me, saying that he didn't need my dumb giants or me. He felt powerful enough. And look, he now lies under the sand and the earth.'

Prahlad could feel the tension in her voice. He continued eating. Her words had stirred some ideas in his head, which he planned to discuss with Dhriti later.

Later that night, Prahlad lay bare-chested next to Dhriti. They were mostly quiet, but Prahlad told her in bursts about what had transpired during the meal and what Maitali had said. Finally, there was silence between them.

'She seems as perturbed by Narasimha and Vaashkal as you.'

'Yes,' he said. 'But her ego stands in the way now. She can help us out, but she doesn't want to. It's her way of spitting on my father's grave. She was always someone who had problems with being too high-minded.'

Dhriti kissed him on the cheek. 'What are you thinking? I know something is going on in your head.'

Prahlad looked around the room, especially the window, from where he feared his words could escape and reach Vaashkal's supporters. 'I am thinking of asking the Danavs for help in taking down Narasimha.'

'Will they agree to do so?'

'I don't know,' Prahlad said. 'I can try to convince them. They have made up their minds to leave, but I know that only they can make it work. They can fight Narasimha, maybe even destroy him.'

'What do you think they will want in return?'

'His head. They want vengeance. It might help if I manage to convince them that Hiranyakashyap's death needs to be avenged.'

Dhriti continued to stare at him. 'I think it's a good idea. You should try it.'

Prahlad smiled. He could feel in his chest that the shackles of prison were beginning to break.

CHAPTER TWENTY-TWO

Indra had always been wary of Brihaspati's anger.

Indra and his army were just a day away from the sea. Sensing that everyone was exhausted, and aware that they had a big battle ahead of them, he asked everyone to halt and take a break.

Ever since the assassination attempt, Indra had had more guards around him. He had brought back his wine tasters to ensure he wasn't poisoned. Brihaspati, Sachi and Vayu were very concerned about Indra and repeatedly asked him if he was okay.

But Indra doubted everyone, especially Brihaspati. An incident from the past had led Indra to suspect that Brihaspati might have had something to do with the assassination attempt.

Indra was trying to forget something he had been forced to remember. He called the old man to his tent, to drink some mead with him, while Vayu prepared the soldiers and Sachi plucked flowers from the field.

Brihaspati had sensed that something was wrong. As soon as he sat down, Indra asked, 'Who do you think has the guts to try and have me assassinated?'

Brihaspati, with his white-as-snow brows and egg-shaped head, said, 'Your Highness, it could be Narasimha.'

'He's not the kind of man who will assassinate someone. He will come out in front and kill his enemy. This attempt ... this was a cowardly move by a desperate person.' Indra looked at the old man in front of him, noticing his reaction. 'What do you think, guruji? I always ask for your guidance. And I need it now more than ever.'

Brihaspati was the guru of the Devas. They used to turn to him before making the smallest of moves. Indra had started to resent this dependency, which Brihaspati had begun to use to his advantage. Indra ensured that the other Devas noticed this as well, leaving Brihaspati angry and frustrated. The old man had never cribbed about this, but it had become a point of hostility between Indra and Brihaspati.

'It's a strange thing. I am quite astounded myself.' Brihaspati was a little lost. Over a hundred years old, he now felt less like a man and more like a soul walking the streets. His guidance was not sought any more. His problems with memory and words only compounded the problem. He knew Indra thought he was mad. Also, he realized that he had been called in just then only for the sake of it. Indra, he thought, would have doubted him more had it not been for his age.

But ... you never knew.

'Yes, indeed. You know, I was recalling our lives. We have had a long association. Now we both are old and grey.' Indra smiled, holding up his cup of mead. 'Cheers to that.'

The old man chuckled nervously and raised his cup.

Indra, meanwhile, could not get Brihaspati's harsh words and his taut stick out of his head.

When Indra was eleven years old, Brihaspati was a young sage, and the only constants in his training were dust and blood. All he heard from the sage was: 'You can never be a king. Look at you. You are such a wimp.'

Saying this, Brihaspati had brought his bamboo stick down on Indra's red buttocks. The little boy, naked and embarrassed, had continued to practice summoning thunder. He had been failing miserably that day.

'Your father didn't sacrifice everything for you to be so useless,' Brihaspati had said to Indra.

Brihaspati had been quite rash with his words back then.

Indra, on the verge of tears, had almost broken down. 'Please don't. I want to rest ... I need water.'

Brihaspati had pushed him to the ground and brought the stick down on his chest as Indra choked and coughed. 'Tell me, do you want to be the king of the Devas?' he had thundered.

'Y-yes.'

'Will you become one if you behave like this? You need to be strong. You cannot fail.'

Indra had looked up at Brihaspati and noticed that the sage was enjoying torturing him. There was sadism on his face, a smile at seeing the troubled boy. Indra didn't understand why he was being such a sadist. What fun was he getting out of it?

'Kashyapa told me that you are the future of Illavarti. How will you live up to his words like this? You are foreigners. You all come from outside. You don't belong to this land, yet he chose you, you little piece of shit.' He had spat on the boy. 'And now I have to make a man out of you, that too when I don't have much to work with here.'

Indra had been tired. He had felt disturbed, as if all his hopes and dreams had been shattered. He was unhappy.

He was not content.

At that time, Indra had taken a vow. He had vowed to take revenge on the old man.

Years had passed since then, but Indra had not forgotten how Brihaspati had tortured him.

He remembered everything. Over time, Indra became powerful. He learnt how to wield the Vajra. He learnt how to control thunder. He became smarter.

Indra had defeated Vatapi, an Asura warlord who was one of the early invaders from Pataal, before Hiranyaksha and Hiranyakashyap had appeared on the scene. Indra and the other Devas had been tasked with ensuring that Vatapi was defeated. They had fought bravely, losing many men in the process, but they were finally triumphant. Celebrations had followed, with kind words and goodwill all around. The people had been happy.

Indra had organized a huge feast and sent out invitations to everyone. He had noticed Varuna and Vayu arguing close to the mead buckets. He had seen Agni in one corner, enjoying the mutton, and the rest of his guests in a good mood. There had been hundreds of people there: Kinnaras, Apsaras, Yakshas. Indra, who was known for his grand celebrations, wasn't married to Sachi back then. He enjoyed the company of women, who lay before him, letting him kiss them.

Somebody had offered him grapes and apricots. There had been a tambourine playing and the Apsaras had been dancing. The white marble had been glistening. Everything had been fantastic. Everything had been beautiful.

Except one thing.

One person had not been invited. Brihaspati.

And yet the sage had come to the celebration, entering as though he had been invited. Indra had looked at him and grinned, descending from his throne and meeting everyone, shaking hands before reaching Brihaspati.

'Thank you so much for coming,' Indra had said.

'Of course, Your Highness.' Brihaspati no longer looked like a stern taskmaster. Instead, he was smiling warmly.

'You told me a long time ago that I was not fit to be a king. Because I am an outsider, a foreigner,' Indra had said with a chuckle. 'I believe you have been proved wrong.'

Brihaspati had raised his eyebrows. 'Oh, Your Highness, it was just to spite you so you would be more motivated to fight.'

'Ah.' Indra had grinned.

'And I believe it worked.' Brihaspati's warm smile had been replaced by a plastic one.

No. It gave me serious insecurities. Indra's nostrils had flared.

'Without me, Your Highness, you wouldn't have been able to fight the Asuras with such ease,' Brihaspati had said confidently. 'I'm glad I was able to help.'

Indra had clenched his jaw. He had wanted to gloat, but the sage had been as arrogant as ever. Indra had turned around and headed back to the pedestal on which his throne sat. He had brought his cup of mead forward and announced, his voice fiery with rage: 'The battle with Vatapi has been a great challenge for us. But we did it with ease because I was supported by the right people, helped by the right people, and because I fought bravely. I would like to call on to this pedestal the people who have been with me through this tough journey. This celebration is for them. Please come …'

With that, Indra had started announcing the names of lords, ministers and Devas, all of whom had stepped up on to the pedestal with humility to accept the honour.

Finally, Indra had glanced at Brihaspati, who had looked shocked. He was the only one Indra hadn't invited on the pedestal.

Anger bubbling within him, Brihaspati had stormed out.

Indra had smiled. He could see that everyone had noticed how Brihaspati had been slighted. He knew no one would mess with him now.

But what had happened after that was something Indra had always wanted to talk to Brihaspati about.

And he planned to do so now.

'The Vatapi incident, the celebration after that …' Indra smiled. 'I believe you were quite angry with me.'

'The Vatapi incident …' the old man looked confused. Indra could see that Brihaspati was trying hard to remember. 'Ah, yes, indeed.' He frowned and then let out a small chuckle. 'That was quite a show you put on.'

'You always treated me badly when I was a kid, so I had to get back at you, which led you to be angry with me.'

'As one should. You were arrogant as a ruler. You thought you were the only one who was always right,' said Brihaspati.

'Do you remember what happened after that?'

'What?'

'A bunch of Asuras attacked us unexpectedly the morning after the celebration. I investigated and found that you had called off the morning patrol for some reason.'

'Because your soldiers were drunk on wine and victory. The patrol would have been useless.' Brihaspati sounded irritated. 'I recall clearly that they were not in any position to head out for a patrol, which was why I asked them to rest. How would I have known that the Asuras would use that as a moment to attack?'

Quite a coincidence.

Indra continued to stare at Brihaspati, his eyes searing through the sage's spirit.

'Oh dear, you don't think I let them in?' Brihaspati chuckled. 'Come on, Your Highness, we might have had a tiff, but I never went against the empire of the Devas.'

'Indeed. And yet you counselled them?'

'I counselled all the children of Kashyapa, which was why he revered me. Please do not think my loyalties lie anywhere else.'

Indra knew that if he was able to connect Brihaspati to the Vatapi incident, he could have linked the sage to the assassination attempt as well. But since he wasn't sure anymore, he didn't want to say anything. He wanted to ensure that the mastermind behind the attack got no warning.

'I understand your scepticism. I know that we have had our ups and downs, but I loved your daughter like my own. We may not have been on the same page always, but I have always respected and adored you,' Brihaspati continued. 'I also understand why you are bringing up past demons. You have just been attacked and are confused about whom to trust. I'm a likely candidate for suspicion, but believe me when I say that I am not responsible. And I am at fault, too. I was cruel to you back in the day because I was xenophobic as a young man. I was not ready to accept that someone from a foreign land could come and rule this country, but I believe Kashyapa made the right decision. So, please accept my humble apology.'

Indra shook his head. He felt defeated. All he wanted to do was to embrace the old sage, which he did. 'My age has made me realize that we were both at fault. I more than you. Thank you for being here. I believe it's long overdue.'

Brihaspati smiled. He returned the embrace.

Indra didn't believe the old sage completely, but at least they had had a conversation. Brihaspati had motivation for sure, but Indra had no proof just then.

And, for some reason, Indra believed that Brihaspati had been honest with him. As the old sage left the tent, Indra knew whom he had to question next, before they headed towards the sea and tried to find the serpent whose belly held the magical bones.

He had to question Sachi, the woman he loved.

CHAPTER TWENTY-THREE

Narasimha set on fire the pyre of his friend—Garuda.

He had never thought that he would have to let go of the few people that he trusted in this kingdom of betrayers and backstabbers, that too so unexpectedly.

First, Prahlad had betrayed him.

And now Garuda was gone.

Narasimha panicked. He felt cornered. He felt like he was being hunted down. The day he had found out … He had locked himself in his room and cried. He had stared out of his window to try and identify who was trying to kill him.

I have enemies.

He had drunk mead and wine till his stomach hurt and his head hung loosely.

And now, on this misty morning, the Suparn chief was being cremated before his eyes. After Garuda, the Suparns had elected another chief, but Narasimha didn't trust him. They were, however, still part of the war because they respected Garuda.

Garuda had come often, asking to meet me ... but I hadn't listened. I wish I had. I should be careful.

Nara wasn't wearing his mane, and he wasn't intoxicated. He was just staring into the darkness in front of him as the fire leapt up towards the sky that was filled with smoke. The people around him, his so-called friends and well-wishers, were staring at the flames too. The shaman had told Narasimha that Garuda had been poisoned.

Poisoned.

Lost in his thoughts, worried, Nara recalled his escapades with Garuda. He remembered how they had got away from Naaglok and how Garuda had saved him from Hiranyakashyap in the nick of time. Narasimha wondered how wrong he had been to think of Garuda as a bad person, even though he had been good and supportive. He had problems regarding his mother. He wanted her ashes. That adventure was in itself a strange altercation.

'One can never be certain about how long one will live.' Nara swivelled his head to see who had said that.

It was Vaashkal. His hair was whipped back with a certain finesse and a sombre smile was dancing on his lips.

Was he behind Garuda's death?

It could be anyone, Nara reminded himself, trying to rein in his emotions. 'I didn't know you were good friends with Garuda.'

'Oh, I was not. He held me responsible for a lot of things, but he needed to realize that I am the only one who likes to see you as king. He thought I had ulterior motives behind believing in you.' Vaashkal shrugged. 'Take the murder of the Asura couple, for instance.'

'Yes. He thought you wanted to stir up the fact that I am against the Asuras. To create more problems for me,' Nara said. 'He thought you ordered their killings.'

'Dead men don't tell stories, I believe.'

'If you were behind any of this, and if I catch a whiff of it, your head will be sliced open in a second.' Nara growled. 'I hope you realize that.'

Vaashkal felt a flicker of fear looking at Narasimha. 'Have I gone against you till now? You have got the public's support. You have more power than you can imagine. I have been nothing but a blessing for you.'

That was true. In fact, it was the only reason why Nara was quiet.

'The Asuras respect strength. Eighty per cent of the population in Kashyapuri and its neighbouring allied states is composed of the Asuras. You have earned their respect. Why, you may ask. Well, because they value your strength, your reliability and your choice of violence over peace. They care about you. They look at you as a leader. Unlike you tribals, we aren't xenophobic. We accept all good and necessary change. Don't you agree?'

Nara shook his head. 'You talk about politics at a funeral. I do not wish to speak to you further.'

'Oh, but you should, my lord. Look around,' Vaashkal said, letting his eyes wander around the field where the ministers, noblemen and merchants stood. They had come for Garuda. 'You have enemies who caused your good friend's death, who wish for your death as well. You need to start thinking about what to do with them before they start planning your death. This death was executed using wolfsbane. What do you think is next? Aconite? It can paralyse you and make you suffer.'

Vaashkal paused and took a deep breath. His voice was as cold as the chill in the air. 'I have worked too hard for you to let you die. We need a plan of action.'

Nara looked at the noblemen and ministers, his eyes uncertain and the worry evident on his face.

'Do you dream well? Do you not let it consume you thinking perhaps there will be someone holding a knife to you?'

'Maybe,' Nara said. 'But, you know, I cannot be killed,' he added with a smirk.

'But you can be gravely wounded and paralysed. Killing is the easiest exit from this world, my lord. If killing was the way of this world, it would be a better place. But that is not the case. Your killers will have plans to make you suffer.'

Nara nodded and spoke through clenched teeth. 'Fine. I get it. What do you have in mind?'

Parvati had decided to travel to Shiva's fort with the Matrikas, while moving back from her journey towards Kashyapuri. It would be on the way and would offer access to a medic, food and an armoury with ease. They needed weapons. Shiva's fort would be ideal for them.

However, Parvati had memories attached to the fort. Her husband used to live there. She, too, had lived there for many years, hiding in the house. When she had set out to find the

Matrikas, Parvati had had no idea if she would ever return, but she did.

That chapter of her life was over. She wanted to move on.

As she entered the fort, the guards greeted her with bows and smiles. She was considered a kind and grateful person. Walking inside, Parvati noticed the stables, the cooks and the small houses where the low-borns worked. There were soldiers around, but not the kind you would expect to see at a royal hall. They displayed raw grit, and they smelled. In fact, a lot of smells assailed Parvati's nose: from human waste to the smells of iron and sulphur.

She moved slowly, bowing to all the people who bowed to her. They seemed apprehensive of the group that followed her, but she knew it was all right because they were with her.

At the end of the market, her eyes fell on the Shiva. He was wearing the emblem of a trishul on his chest, along with heavy armour, a long coat and a smile on his face. He was Bhairav's right-hand man, his go-to person. Veerbhadra.

Parvati was given a shawl as she sneezed. Sitting before a fire, she realized how exhausted she was as she drank tulsi tea. She almost felt as if she was home. She smiled as Veerbhadra got himself some mead and sat opposite her, the orange flames lighting up his face. 'My lady, it's a surprise, truly,' he said.

'I'm not a lady anymore,' Parvati said with a weak smile. 'I am just another woman.'

He shook his head. 'If only that were true.' And then, after a pause, he asked, 'So how come you are here? An odd job?'

She shook her head. Since the Matrikas were resting for the night, Parvati and Veerbhadra had a chance to catch up.

'How is the title of Shiva treating you?'

Veerbhadra shrugged. 'I don't know. It's tough. I just … sometimes I feel I was not the right choice.'

'Oh, not this again. Bhairav specifically chose you as his successor.'

'Because I was loyal to him,' Veerbhadra said. 'Not because I was the right choice.'

'And who, according to you, would have been the right choice?'

'You.'

Parvati froze for a second. 'What?'

'He wanted you to lead the fort. The north, actually.' Letting out a sigh, he sipped from the cup. 'But he didn't do it because you were already so burdened by the pressure of Bhringi's passing that you didn't seem ready for anything new at that point.'

'But why did he think I was the right choice?'

'Have you seen yourself, my lady? You are a powerful woman. You are decisive and intelligent enough to know when to speak up and when to keep your own counsel. You are kind and you haven't let the world corrupt you. Instead, you are the type of person who ensures the world is a little kinder than it was yesterday. That's a sign of a good leader.' Veerbhadra smiled. 'And now, here we are. You are back in action, out there in the world for something—I have no idea what it is—but you are fighting and haven't given up.'

Parvati nodded. She couldn't believe she was hearing all of this. 'Um, thank you.'

'Do you ever think of coming back here?'

'Not really.'

'You should. At least I'll be relieved of my duty that way. I want to hand over all responsibility to you, but whenever you are ready. I was planning to send you a raven to convey this message, but then I didn't know where to send it. You keep travelling.'

Parvati let out a small chuckle. 'Veer, thank you so much for the offer, but I would like you to execute all the duties of being the Shiva. And do not fret. You are doing a wonderful job.'

Veerbhadra smiled back.

The two of them looked at the flames, which didn't look fiery that night. They were, in fact, a symbol of peace.

The Matrikas had been travelling for a while since they left Shiva's fort. Parvati had got herself a spear—long and serrated. She practiced wielding it every day against the trunk of a peepul tree, trying to get a better hold on it.

However, their journey back home wasn't so simple. Especially once they learnt about the letter and what it said ...

All of them had first debated the contents of the letter within their own minds and then spoken to each other. They didn't want to share their thoughts with Parvati yet, but Parvati knew something was brewing.

One day, while they were having lunch, the Matrikas approached Parvati.

'The women are talking,' Brahmani said.

Parvati was having mushroom soup. 'And what would that be about?'

'They think we should not kill Andhaka. That we should try to reform him.'

Parvati's eyebrows shot up. 'Are you joking? Have you forgotten that he killed one of our own? He killed my husband. That man ...' she paused, realizing she didn't need to defend herself so vehemently. 'Where is this coming from?'

'The fact that he's Skanda. Even Hiranyaksha believed it,' said Brahmani matter-of-factly. 'I also think he's the one. He was born from your womb.'

Parvati clenched her jaw. 'I know the odds are against us, but he doesn't behave like Skanda. I do not think we should spare him. He's beyond saving, and I really don't care.'

'He's your son,' Brahmani added.

Parvati chuckled. 'If he was my son, he wouldn't have thrown us to the Vaitarli. He would have shown us that he still had some compassion and humanity left in him.'

'He can be saved. We will help him. We will be his mothers. Let's give him a chance.'

Parvati shook her head. 'I'm sorry, but that's not possible. He has to die. I will ensure that.'

Brahmani's nostrils flared. 'I obeyed you as we travelled all over, I jumped and fought when you wanted me to. I led our team till you came along, letting you take over because I accepted you as our leader, but you can't just dismiss all ideas opposed to yours like a tyrant. You need to realize that there are other perspectives that need to be respected.'

Parvati didn't say anything. She calmly went about enjoying her lunch, ignoring Brahmani, who left in a huff.

Parvati remembered the day she had found those books that her guru had tried to hide. She had seen names. They were names of people she never thought existed. And that's why Parvati knew that Andhaka was not Skanda, because she remembered. There had been Matrikas before Parvati and her team. She knew there had been a group of women who had fought and trained under the guru, but that the local king had not been encouraging.

Parvati wanted to tell Brahmani this, but she wasn't sure. A name had stuck with her all this while. A name she thought she remembered.

To be honest, she had never been too sure if a person by that name even existed. And if that was the case, she knew who the real Skanda was.

A council meeting was set up.

Narasimha sat at the head of the long table that overlooked the pedestal where all the ministers, noblemen and princes of the allied states were sitting. They had been summoned into the city hall for a meeting, but they had not been informed of the purpose. Nara had been exceptionally silent.

Everyone was worried. Nara could see the concern on their faces, but he still kept quiet. Vaashkal stepped on to the pedestal and came to the front. The murmurs continued.

Finally, the doors of the hall were locked. Everyone fell silent and exchanged looks.

'Thank you so much for coming, everyone,' Vaashkal began. 'Ever since Lord Narasimha took over after Hiranyakashyap, we have been winning wars. The kingdom has grown from strength to strength. Our economy, too, is recovering. Soon, Illavarti will also be ours—our campaign against Indra will continue at Amravati. As per the last information we received, Indra is headed for the sea. One might wonder why. Maybe he fears us. Our army will attack his soldiers there.'

Vaashkal kept speaking, his voice taking on a menacing tone. 'That said, we are in a strange situation. I believe a lot of you are against Narasimha, that you are critical of his rule. I believe we can use this pedestal to talk about it. Lord Narasimha, being the benevolent king that he is, wants to hear your plight and your perspective. He wants to hear what you have in mind to ensure that the empire grows. It would be best if you get your questions and statements to us, so that Lord Narasimha can address them.'

Nobody stood up. There was complete silence.

Narasimha spoke up. 'Please do not hesitate. Whoever thinks I can do better should come forward. I am more than happy to address all concerns and questions.'

The members of the audience looked around, confused. Was this happening for real? Did the king really want to hear them out?

Yet, no one stood up.

Nara picked up a piece of paper. 'I believe I have the names of people who were against me when Prahlad, the son of the late Hiranyakashyap, wanted to take the helm from me. I have the list, so it is best they stand up and speak to me directly, rather than plot behind my back. It will be best for both of us … because if I start naming from the list, it won't be good.'

A murmur ran through the audience.

Nara waited. He waited long enough, until he felt his mind was going around in circles thinking about the cowardly act that was being planned here. 'Fine, I'm starting with the names. When I call them out, stand up.'

Nara began. He took the first name.

A man stood up meekly. He was a moneylender from the east, an Asura, who stood silently. Before he could explain himself, an arrow slammed into his skull. He fell to the ground.

There were no more whispers. Everybody stood up as guards circled them, ensuring no one could leave. The gates had already been closed.

'For those who supported me, do not fret. Your names will not be called out. For those who didn't, stand up now.' Nara noticed several people sitting down. He reminded them of the consequence of lying to him.

Everyone feared for their safety. Some were even whimpering.

Narasimha called out another name. And then another. The list in Nara's hands had been put together by Vaashkal and supplemented by a few of his loyal ministers.

As the names were called out, the men stood up and fell prey to the arrows. By the time Nara got to the end of the list, there were twenty corpses on the ground.

'Anyone else who wants to speak? Now is your chance. I will forgive you.'

This time, five men stood up. They were those who didn't agree with all of Nara's policies.

'Wonderful. I'm glad you had the courage to stand up, even though your friends lie dead right here.' And then he smiled. 'I believe you will be happy with them.'

Everyone was confused for a second. But that was only until five arrows came out of nowhere and the five men fell instantly.

Nara wore his mane, which he had not put on till now. He walked to the edge of the pedestal, his body massive and his fingers crackling with electricity.

'Remember this day, those of you who have survived,' Nara said. Many of the noblemen and ministers were crying. Some of them were on their knees, bowing to him out of fear. 'Those who go against me shall perish, and those who stand with me shall forever earn riches.'

The audience chanted in unison: 'LORD NARASIMHA! LORD NARASIMHA!'

Nara smiled. He had never felt so powerful. It was addictive.

Parvati was about to sleep when the Matrikas came to her. They had still not reached Kashyapuri.

'We would like to speak to you,' they said.

Parvati rolled her eyes. 'I know what this is about. Please do not irritate me. Get some sleep.'

Chamundi spoke up. 'You need to realize, Parvati, that we also have a choice here. As Matrikas promised to the code and our brethren, we will help Skanda no matter what. He's our child, too. He must be protected.'

'You don't understand. It's more complicated than that,' Parvati said. 'You will be protecting an insane man.'

'We will help him reform,' Narasimhi said. 'He will be fine. He just needs enough time.'

Parvati stood up, annoyed. She saw Brahmani standing quietly at the back. Shoving her way past the others, she said, 'If you have something to say, talk to me. Don't influence everyone.'

'It's a unilateral decision,' Brahmani said.

'We have been going strong till now. Why did you involve the others? Why did you complicate everything? We have a mission ... to kill Andhaka ... and now that is changing.'

Brahmani shrugged. 'We have gone through the worst with you, and we will continue to support you, Parvati. But you have to listen to us. You can't shut us down.'

'I agree,' Parvati began.

Might as well tell them the truth.

'After Chenchen went to Nrriti, she informed me about their conversation. Nrriti especially mentioned that Skanda is not who you think he is. It is someone unexpected, someone who will emerge as a hero. I have had my doubts ever since. I wondered who it could be. I wondered if I was missing something obvious. I kept going back in time, searching through my memories. And then I remembered. Before us, there was one more Matrika, someone who was unsuccessful,' Parvati said with a sigh.

She continued. 'You know that the Matrikas before us comprised both Asura women and tribals. Our guru preached to the Asuras. Some of the women believed him and joined him. It was from this group that some were chosen to be Matrikas.'

'What does this have to do with anything?' Brahmani asked.

The fire was burning, the logs were crackling.

Parvati pursed her lips. 'Among those royal Asura women was someone we have all heard of, someone who was the reason behind the wars in this country, who was selected as a Matrika but chose to leave.' She looked at the other Matrikas. They gasped as she spoke next.

'Kayadhu,' Parvati said. 'Prahlad's mother.'

CHAPTER TWENTY-FOUR

Indra had reached the docks with his army.

Before them were a medley of longships, a trader's market and fishermen with their nets. The smell of small fish hung in the air. There were scallops being sold and oysters being cooked. The fishermen noticed the king and his army. Some of them bowed, welcoming them, while others turned away. They had expected it, for scouts had visited the docks earlier to ensure it was safe for the king and to prepare the ships.

Indra knew where to go; his daughter's sketch had indicated the spot. They had to move towards the Black Ocean, also called the Dark Bay. Indra was waiting by the docks, taking in the saline smell and the loud squawking of the seagulls in the distance, when Sachi came up to him. Indra looked at the longships being prepared.

'You called me?' she asked.

Once a gorgeous woman, her oval face was now masked by creases and wrinkles. Though Indra still considered her beautiful, he remembered how voluptuous she had been when they first met. Her eyes, however, were still a striking gold.

She was a mother now. And, of course, a wife. The exhaustion was visible on her face. Indra knew that both of them were emotionally spent after losing their two children. While Sachi had expressed her grief through silence, Indra had decided to travel to the edge of the world to retrieve the bones of a sage from a mythical serpent's stomach.

Both had to do damage control.

'I'm lost. I don't know if I'm doing the right thing. The people are not happy,' Indra said. 'I'm afraid of what might happen if the journey doesn't yield anything.'

'You are listening to your daughter,' Sachi said. 'And remember that she was a child. I understand why you are doing this, but you shouldn't have dragged everyone here. Amravati is unguarded right now. It can be attacked.'

'You think we should return?' Indra was still trying to gauge if Sachi would have wanted to see him dead for undertaking this voyage, for leaving Amravati.

Sachi looked at her husband of many years. She knew the man inside out. 'This situation reminds me of something from a long time back. When we both were young and our bones were tough, but our minds had strayed.'

'What?'

'The Nahusha episode.'

The head of Vritra, the dragon, was shown to the people. Everyone had rejoiced. Vritra's reign of terror had ended.

Indra had slain him with his Vajra. There had been jubilation all around.

Indra, however, had stood at the banks of the river, which was finally free of Vritra's control. He had been looking at it, and it had pearls he noticed under the dying sun.

'What happened?' Sachi had asked. She had been young, happy and pregnant. She had moved closer to her husband, confused about why he was sad. 'What happened to you?' she had asked.

'I am not happy.'

'Well, you should be. You saved our people.'

'Yes, but I also killed a child.'

'What do you mean?'

'This was Tvastr's baby. He had created Vritra using his own hands, and now I have killed him. I shamed him when he had given me control over the Vajra. And I shamed him even further. I killed him.' Indra shook his head in disappointment. 'Because I knew if I didn't slay him, he would have come at me. Again. And again. I killed him even though I didn't want to.'

'But you did it for your people.'

'Is killing one for the sake of many justified?'

Sachi hadn't known what to say. Indra had turned around and looked at the people celebrating excitedly.

'I'm leaving,' Indra had said.

'Where are you going?'

'I don't know.'

'What do you mean? You can't just leave.'

Indra hadn't listened to her. He had walked into the river. 'I'll return, don't worry.'

'I'm pregnant. I am carrying twins … you can't just …'

But Indra had gone.

Sachi had been alone for months after that. In Indra's absence, Amravati had needed a new king. While the other Devas had strongholds in other parts of the country, Nahusha, a young Manav king with many children and many yagnas to his name, had been appointed the temporary ruler. He had been a handsome man—tall and slender with short hair.

Sachi, however, was still the queen. Nahusha made life hell for her. He would taunt and tease her, flirt with her without caring that she was another man's wife.

In fact, once when he had cornered her, Sachi had had to hit him to remind him that she was not his wife.

Indra stared at Sachi. He was doing what he had done in the past. It was a pattern.

'You know what happened after that,' Sachi said. 'Nahusha from the Aila dynasty was crowned as the king of Amravati, as other Devas cannot be that. He rallied support, made advances at me and behaved like a tyrant. You left the kingdom in disarray. You returned after three months, after the birth of your children. You ousted Nahusha, took most of his land back and forced him to leave Illavarti.'

Indra remembered. He had gone away because he wanted to repent. He wanted to go to Kailash and meditate to forget everything.

'You are right,' he said finally. 'I shouldn't have done that. I can't just leave and jeopardize everyone's safety. Do you think this is the reason someone wants to have me killed?'

'You are a king. You can be assassinated for far smaller things.'

Indra chuckled and hugged Sachi. 'You are probably right. I might seem like an escapist, but I'm telling you that this is real. I'm sure we will find something out there.'

'I hope so too.'

'Do you despise me?'

'For what?'

'For what happened to Jayanti.'

Sachi's eyebrows shot up, but she didn't say anything.

'I feel we have become colder towards each other since her death. I think you blame me for her death,' Indra said.

Sachi sighed. 'What do you want me to say? Do you want me to lie, or do you want the truth?'

'I have never wanted you to lie to me.'

'Now, that's not true,' Sachi shook her head and said. 'Jayanti died because of your pursuit for revenge. You have always been a scornful man. You have kept grudges when you shouldn't have. If someone slaps you, you don't ignore it or slap that person back. Instead, you stab him. Now, I knew the man I was getting married to, but I never knew that our children would have to face danger because of this attitude. You need to understand that if someone slaps you, it is all right to retreat. If the person attacks again, retreat a little more. Remember, revenge is best served cold. That's how it should be.'

Indra knew that Sachi was not trying to hurt him, but he felt guilty. His daughter had died because of his quest for revenge. He could have handled the situation better. He should not have killed Chenchen and Narasimha's child. He could have spoken to Narasimha, or they could have duelled. There were so many options, so many ways to avoid doing what he had done.

Indra realized that this journey he had undertaken could lead to his damnation. But despite knowing that he had gone ahead with it.

After talking to his wife, he was seeing things from another perspective. Perhaps he had been wrong in bringing everyone along with him.

Perhaps he should stop.

Or perhaps …

CHAPTER TWENTY-FIVE

In Hiranyapur, Prahlad was preparing for a trial.

It wasn't a trial that would decide his fate, but the kind where giant heads would be looking at him as he tried to convince them not to leave. He had already convinced Maitali to grant him a session with the giants, as a gesture of farewell, but she didn't know that Prahlad had more planned.

Neither did Shantaram.

Prahlad wanted to keep it that way. He wanted to say goodbye, but he wanted to say a little more as well. He knew that if Shantaram attended the session, he would attack him, or maybe even kill him. It was a risk Prahlad was willing to take.

As he buttoned up his sherwani and looked at his reflection in the water, Dhriti came up from behind.

'Are you sure about this?' she asked.

'I am.'

'What if they don't agree? Narasimha will not give you another chance.'

'I don't need it,' Prahlad said. 'I know for sure that I can make this work for both of us. I am prepared to go to war against Narasimha.'

Prahlad, with his shabby hair and darker-than-usual eyes, was serious. He was worried, too. He didn't want to see a disappointed look on Narasimha's face again, but then he looked at the ring on his finger. He was doing this for the right reasons; he was doing what Lord Vishnu would have wanted him to do.

It was a rainy day. The pedestal had been placed inside the citadel. It was a circular arrangement, with a ceiling that opened up to the skies. But instead of clouds, all Prahlad could see were the heads of the giants, rain and mist clouding their faces, their eyes glowering. A simple movement from any of them caused the pedestal to tremble.

Inside the citadel, in the shadows where the standing lamps burnt, were other people—the soldiers, Maitali, Dhriti, Shantaram and Narayana. They were all waiting for Prahlad to begin his address.

Dhriti was carefully positioned behind Shantaram.

Maitali stepped on to the pedestal and looked up. The rain lashed at her face. 'Today, we have with us Prahlad, son of Hiranyakashyap, the king who was killed. Prahlad wants to wish us well before we undertake our journey tomorrow. He has come to say goodbye.'

Before a nervous Prahlad (for the giants were intimidating) could come up and speak, a booming voice asked, 'Why should we listen to him? He defied his own bloodline.'

The giant's voice echoed inside the chambers, sending fear down everyone's spine.

'Because we worship strength. And he has shown great strength today by coming here, and earlier by defying his father who had strayed.' There was a slight note of warmth in Maitali's voice.

There was no response from the giants. Maitali nodded to Prahlad, giving him his cue to speak.

Prahlad was wearing his gloves. He knew he had to choose his words carefully. 'I stand before you today, Great Ones. You, the Danavs, have always been considered, according to my nan, a true testament to strength. You stayed in Illavarti because of my father. You did not care about petty politics. You followed my father because he was a good man, a strong man. And yes, it is true that he had strayed and needed to be stopped.'

The giants sighed. To Prahlad, it was a loud noise.

'I let my father die in front of my eyes, I defied my bloodline as you clearly said, because he had been corrupted. I placed Narasimha, a god, in his place. I had hoped that such a situation would not recur, but things are changing. Recently, I was informed that Narasimha has killed several of his ministers, those who held opinions contrary to his. He's an Avatar of Vishnu, but perhaps he has forgotten that. To defeat him, I need someone equally powerful.'

'What are you doing?' Shantaram asked loudly.

Prahlad ignored him. 'I invite you,' he yelled loudly under the rain, 'to help me get rid of this monster. I invite you to fight him. I cannot defeat him alone; I need all the help I can get. I need to restore peace and bring back the golden age.'

The giants were quiet, but Shantaram grabbed his sword and began moving towards Prahlad. Dhriti intercepted him and brought out a knife, but he pushed her away. Shantaram and his soldiers jumped on to the pedestal.

'I told you not to act funny,' Shantaram said to Prahlad.

Prahlad stared at Maitali, who was trying to understand what was happening, but Shantaram's soldiers surrounded her.

'You did it. You defied him. I was given clear instructions— kill on sight.' Shantaram grinned as he raised his sword.

Prahlad deflected it with a blade that he had hidden on his person. They parried and swung as the storm above grew thicker and the thunder crackled. The eyes of the giants continued to glower even more.

'You cannot stop me. I will make sure he's dethroned,' Prahlad said to Shantaram.

'You are an idiot. And idiots don't deserve to be given another chance to live.'

Prahlad glanced at Dhriti, who was fighting a bunch of soldiers alone, while Maitali had been grabbed and pushed against the floor.

'This is tyranny, Shantaram. You are a good man and I don't want to hurt you.'

'In a duel, there is no good or bad man. There's just an enemy. You are my enemy.'

Their swords clanged. And then Shantaram kicked Prahlad in the gut, making him fall. Prahlad breathed deeply.

'You are going to lose, amateur. It's the end for you,' said Shantaram.

He had his sword pointed at Prahlad when a shadow came over them. Both Prahlad and Shantaram looked up. A large hand grabbed a screaming Shantaram, raised him high and then cast him aside like an ant.

One of the giants had come to Prahlad's rescue.

A shocked Prahlad stared at what was happening around him.

'Leave our preceptor, or face our wrath,' one of the giant boomed. Shantaram's soldiers moved away from Dhriti and Maitali.

'We hate distractions during a conversation,' the giant added.

Prahlad almost found it witty. He smirked and looked up at the sky.

'Yes, continue, boy. Why should we attack Kashyapuri?'

Prahlad swallowed nervously. 'Because it's the right thing to do.'

There was a chuckle in response, one that sounded more like a scoff.

'What do we stand to gain if we help you? Ever since we fought at Illavarti, we have only faced persecution and unsettling weather. We want peace, and here you are asking us to fight. We might win, but at the end of it all we will still wonder what the point was. To conquer Illavarti was never our dream. It was your father and uncle's, and now it is yours.

We listened to your elders because they symbolized strength, but now we ask you—what's the point?'

Prahlad had nothing to offer. He couldn't give them world domination ideas because he was not into world domination. He couldn't offer them resources because they had everything. After all, they wore loincloths in the name of clothes. Prahlad knew he didn't have all the time in the world to answer them, but he had nothing to say.

Finally, he spoke. 'I came to you because of the blood we share. You can leave after that, knowing that you helped someone who has the same blood coursing through his veins,' Prahlad said. 'I want this country to grow, but right now it is perishing. It has become a land of violence.'

There was a long pause before a hum took over.

'We wish you godspeed, boy. But, unfortunately, we do not see the point. We helped your father and we did our bit to help our bloodline. Our prayers are with you.'

The ground shook and the glowering eyes disappeared. Prahlad was left with the clouds over his head. Defeated, he fell down on his knees and sobbed quietly. He had failed. He wanted to call them back.

What about doing the right thing? Was anyone even listening!

'I'm done with this!' Prahlad shouted, throwing away the brass cup in his hand. 'I'm done fighting for a cause. No one cares about the right thing. Everyone wants to benefit, but no one wants to help. First, I went to the ministers, and they said no. Then I went to the giants and they said no. Why? Because they are all selfish. They are only looking out for themselves. No one cares about the country, or about Dharma. Prahlad's eyes were watery.

Dhriti watched him from a distance. She was sad for him. She was trying to be as supportive as she could despite him pushing her away.

'And now I will be hunted and hounded. I will have no choice but to run and hide. I have no hope. What can I do? How can you kill a god? You can't. You can't,' Prahlad lamented. He stood close to a window, looking out at the sandy city of Hiranyapur.

'We should leave,' Dhriti said. 'An emissary has already left for Narasimha. He will be here soon. We will be hunted down if we are still here. In any case, mercenaries will be hired and we will be wanted for treason. We need to make a run for it now.'

Prahlad didn't know what to do. He felt cornered.

'We can ask Maitali if we can go to Pataal with her,' Dhriti said. 'That's our best bet. She will agree. She has to.'

Prahlad shook his head. 'That's no place for us. It's a cold island where the skies are darker than the water surrounding it. I have been dependent on others for far too long. I should have taken action myself.'

Just then, there was a knock on the door. Dhriti opened it, expecting it to be Maitali. But, to Prahlad's surprise, it was none other than Narayana.

'Narayana, how come you are here?'

'I would like to speak to you, Lord Prahlad. In private, if that is all right.'

Prahlad nodded, stepping outside the room, not missing Dhriti's worried face. He knew that she understood how tormented he was feeling.

'Yes, what happened?' Prahlad asked Narayana.

'I couldn't help but be impressed by your willpower, Your Lordship.'

'Thank you.'

'I do not know if this will help, but this was a wrong move in the first place. The giants are lazier than ever. You need to take matters into your own hands.'

'I wish I could. Is this conversation going to be about the things I've done wrong?'

Narayana chuckled nervously. 'No, it's to help you, my lord.'

'And how is that?'

'I do not know how true it is, but if it is, it could benefit you. Since I'm at your service, I should tell you that I've overheard a few merchants from the north. They claim to have heard from the soldiers who guard the underground coves of Shiva's fort that they have seen the Sharabha sword.'

'What is that?'

'Oh, I believe you aren't interested in history. The sword is made from the spine of Shiva, and it is believed that it is the only weapon that can kill an Avatar of Vishnu. I don't know how true it is, or if it even exists, but I think that if you really believe in what you were saying, you will have faith in this information, too. This was a secret until your father, who knew about the sword, spoke about it to everyone. He made jokes about it.'

'Why didn't he believe in it?'

'He didn't believe in Trimurti like I do, my lord.' Narayana's eyes glanced at the ring on Prahlad's finger. 'As do you. If you have faith, you can try to find what you are seeking. I hope the sword helps you.'

Prahlad wanted to go back in time, to visit his father's study and try to find any journals where he may have talked about the sword. But, Prahlad reasoned, if he ridiculed it, he would not have written about it.

'Thank you,' Prahlad said. 'Thank you so much.'

He didn't know whether this sword existed, or if it would work. But he knew that trying to find it was better than going to Pataal.

CHAPTER TWENTY-SIX

Probably a fortnight had gone by. Narasimha's dreams had got better.

He had spent all his waking hours planning an attack on Amravati. He had no clue where Indra was, or what he planned to do. Had he really left? Had he really escaped? Nara had sent scouts, but they were yet to return.

Nara was worried. He wanted to kill Indra. He wanted to see his eyes close forever, but he wasn't sure if he would be able to do it.

The entire city was gripped with fear. The chiefs of others fiefs had come to him for help, to be allies and to give him gold and their daughters. But he had rejected all of it. He only wanted allegiance.

It was probably Vaashkal's doing, Nara thought. He should thank Vaashkal and be grateful to him.

Nara was in the war room when he received the news. He had decided to take a break from drinking.

I have decided. I will live in the fields after this. Once Indra is dead ... or perhaps I'll rule. I'm good at it.

He was lost in his thoughts when the door was flung open and Vaashkal entered without announcing himself. He had a paper in his hand, a scroll of some kind.

'Oh, you would love to hear this. I'm telling you, you should start treating others with cruelty rather than kindness.'

'What happened?'

Vaashkal handed the scroll over to Nara. After reading it, Nara was quiet. He should have been angry, but he had expected it.

'Prahlad betrayed me again.'

'What should we do? Exile him to some place far off?'

'Well, you were the one who told me not to kill him.'

'I was wrong!' Vaashkal spat in anger. 'Only because you were close to the boy, otherwise I would have found a way to burn him alive.'

'Calm down,' Nara said. 'Do me a favour. Send your best soldiers to Hiranyapur and have him killed. Don't bring the corpse here.'

'Oh my! So you are ready to do that?'

'He's a threat to my plans and I have given him enough chances. He didn't appreciate them, so it's best to end him,' Nara said casually.

'I am glad. And I shall do as you ordered. But Prahlad is not in Hiranyapur. No one knows where he is.'

'But the giants ... he probably left with them.'

'That would be a smart move. It doesn't sound like Prahlad.' Vaashkal chuckled. 'Don't worry. I will spread the word—a hundred thousand coins for anyone who gets me his head.

He has become too much of a bother now. And this reward, I shall give it out of my own pocket, not from the treasury.'

'Quite generous of you.'

Nara didn't want to kill Prahlad. All he wanted was Indra's head. 'We should focus on Amravati,' he said.

'The army is ready. We have got fifty per cent more people ready to join the war. Apparently,' Vaashkal said as he walked to the wine cellar and filled two cups, 'your last stint as an honourable king led everyone to follow you blindly.'

'I still think it was too much, but maybe it was necessary.'

'They should fear you.' Vaashkal clenched his fist as he brought the goblet to Nara. 'Here. Cheers to us to finally making tough calls.'

'I am quitting this habit.'

Vaashkal's face went pale. 'Now that is a bother and a shame. I thought we were friends. For old time's sake, just have a last drink.'

'Only one.'

'Only one is needed for the occasion.'

'What is the occasion though?'

'I believe I have never told you much about myself. Well, I am not from a well-off family. We were Asuras, but we were poor. I gained knowledge through libraries and mentors who guided me. But, because of my orange hair and funny face, I faced a lot of ridicule. I was bullied a lot. I learnt a lot on the streets, about human behaviour especially, but it was never enough. I worked for the treasury and different political departments, but I stayed stuck in the shadows. And I hated that. You know what happened then?'

Nara took a sip. The drink had a rough, metallic taste, but he swallowed it. 'What?'

'I met a man. A genius. A visionary. He helped me. He was my hero. When bullies hunted me, he would come and punish them. I looked up to this man. Meanwhile, I developed a fascination for poisons that were fashioned from flowers and vines that were rejected by people, the very people who rejected me.' Vaashkal shook his head. 'And then one day my hero left. We talked over letters and stayed in touch until I learnt the truth.'

'What is that?'

'That I am Hiranyakashyap's son.' Vaashkal smiled.

Nara stopped drinking. 'What?'

'Well, he adopted me. I used to do all his dirty work, things he couldn't do as a king. That's why I was always in the shadows. While he showed himself to be great and mighty, I would handle the rats that plagued the city. When you killed him, I was away on a diplomatic mission. I cried my heart out when I heard the news, but I knew it was for the good of the empire and the country. He had to be put down. After all, someone tougher and stronger than him had become his downfall. And we, as Asuras, worship strength, right?'

Nara could feel his joints loosen a little. His eyes felt sluggish. He didn't know what he was going through, but he was feeling a lot of pain.

What is going on?

'I supported you thinking that it would be best if I stayed in the good books of the man who was all-powerful till my friend returned, as tough as before, to replace you and to become a symbol of the true meaning of strength. And then everyone would follow him. But something like this takes work. It takes a lot of time,' Vaashkal said with a smile.

Nara's grip around the goblet loosened. His eyes widened as the goblet clanged on the ground. 'Who is this man?' he managed to ask.

'It is me. Hmm,' a voice said.

'Andhaka …'

Nara hadn't noticed it, but someone had been standing in the shadows. Whimpering, he fell, unable to move. He was unable to blink or open his mouth. He was paralysed. But he could see, smell and hear. His eyes wandered to the shadows to see a man enter. He was bald, with a tough-looking bare-chested body.

Nara noticed his eyes—the pitch-black eyes, darker than night itself. And his smile was a malicious smile.

'The list that you read out, Lord Narasimha,' Vaashkal said. 'All those names were of the people who were against me. The cabinet and the allies were loyal to you. You helped me execute those who could oppose me. Now you shall rot in prison, while we fulfil what we set out to do. Had you not been an Avatar, you would have been killed.'

Andhaka knelt and played with Nara's hair. 'It's always good to meet you. Hmm. But this time, I have no duplicates with me. It's just me. The real me. I do not need duplicates any more.' With that, Andhaka picked up Nara's heavy body and flung him across the room. 'See how easy it is.'

Nara was paralysed, so he didn't feel pain. But he felt anger and rage. He couldn't do much about it though.

'Remember how I told you about the paralysis … yes, this is aconite. I grow it in my garden. It delivers quite a punch.

It won't kill you, but you will not feel alive either.' Vaashkal clapped his hands to call the guards. 'Please take this wretched man away from my sight.'

They did. They grabbed him by the arms and began carrying him outside when Andhaka stopped them. He walked up to Nara and looked him in the eye.

'It's not Andhaka any more. Hmm,' he said with a smirk. 'It's Skanda.'

CHAPTER TWENTY-SEVEN

If it wasn't Brihaspati, if it wasn't Sachi …

Indra knew who it was. It was clear. It had to be him. Nothing else made sense.

The ships had set sail and the symbol of the elephant on the flags soared high. Indra stood on the hull of one of the ships, looking up. The rain had been incessant and a storm was beginning to brew. There had been a time when he could have controlled these forces, but not any more.

Indra felt powerless. He held the flag in his hand. He could see that he was weak. His hands were shaking. Sachi had called him into the quarterdeck several times, but he had refused. He liked being in the open.

'Brother!' Indra heard a loud cry behind him. He recognized the voice. He had been thinking about this man. 'Come inside. The winds are strong. I tried controlling them, but they are only becoming harsher. Come inside. Your wife calls you.'

Indra turned to see Vayu. He was a beautiful man, younger than him, with short frizzy hair. He was nothing like Agni, who could rattle people. Vayu was the kind of person who knew how to cap his frustrations in.

And that, according to Indra, was the problem.

'It was you, wasn't it?' Indra asked.

'What?'

'You did it. You tried to assassinate me.'

'Are you mad?' Vayu scoffed. 'Why would I do that?'

The storm had picked up, causing the ship to rock. 'Because you never liked me. You never approved of my decisions. You said you did, but you always cursed me behind my back. You would hurt me if you had to.'

'This is not true. I have always respected you.'

'Oh, is that so?' Indra raised his eyebrows. 'I know about the day you went to our father.'

Vayu's expression changed.

Vayu remembered the cove. Beautifully dark yet luminous, a narrow stream teeming with colourful fish flowing inside. Kashyapa sitting in the cove, cross-legged and meditating. He was a huge man, taller than most people. In fact, he was almost a giant. He was sitting there with his hair tied and a small stream of water falling on his head, which he didn't mind. He had a smile dancing on his face.

Vayu had been young then. He hadn't had the goatee he now did. Instead, his face was clean-shaven then.

'Come here, my child. How can I help you?' Kashyapa's voice echoed.

Vayu was always afraid of his father. His daunting appearance intimidated the young Vayu. 'I am confused, father.'

'And you look confused,' Kashyapa said without even opening his eyes. 'What has befuddled you?'

'Agni holds fire. Varuna holds water. Indra holds thunder and the skies. And I …' Vayu narrowed his gaze, 'I hold the bloody wind. What is this? I mean, even Indra can control the wind.'

Kashyapa, with his eyes still closed, had seen through Vayu's confusion. Vayu had always felt that he was Indra's shadow, as a result of which he felt insecure.

'I should have been given something else. Something more.'

'You can't just …' Kashyapa shook his head. 'Why are you having these thoughts, my son? You have been an adulterer all your young life; you have let women influence you.'

Vayu scornfully chuckled. 'You have mistaken me for Indra. He is the one who has no clue about what he wants. He pillages and loots. He lusts and forgets. He's a flawed man. And you made him the king. In fact, you brought Brihaspati to ensure he became the king. This is wrong. Even Varuna would have been a better choice.'

'Yes, he's a flawed man. But remember that only a person who can identify his own issues can correct what is wrong in society,' Kashyapa said. 'You have lived in his shadow, and you will continue to live that way because that is your fate. You will never be heard, not because you won't have good ideas, but because you will not be able to stand up to anyone who has the courage to voice his ideas over yours, even if they are ill-intentioned. Rather than crying about not having enough powers, you should work on taming the winds and bringing them under your control. But what you are doing instead is cribbing about the situation, because you think your father will not say a word.'

Vayu was shocked. Kashyapa, his eyes open now, had been blunt. Vayu had bowed and left the cove—the grudge he held against Indra had become greater.

'Our father told me that you went against me,' Indra shouted as the waves lashed at the ship. 'I never said anything because I thought you would change. But you tried to assassinate me? Because I don't live up to your ideals? Because I don't do what you think is right?'

Vayu stared at Indra in silence. The water was hitting his face hard. 'I didn't do it, brother. And I don't know what I should do to prove it. I might have lived in your shadow, and I may not approve of some of your decisions, but I would never send someone to kill you. If needed, I would do it myself.'

'You are too much of a coward.' Indra laughed.

'You have brought your entire kingdom here on this wild goose chase. You are spoiling the very fabric of what we stand for. We have lost, Devendra! We have lost this war! Like hermits, we have nowhere to go. There are far more powerful people out there right now who can easily defeat us. You have led us to this point. And now, seeing this storm, I believe we all will die,' Vayu shouted. 'All this has happened because you are not a worthy king.'

'If it is so easy to be a king, why don't you try and see things from my perspective?'

'I'm sure I'll do a better job.'

Sachi and Brihaspati had come out with soldiers by now. Sachi ordered the soldiers to step in between the brothers, but Indra raised his hand. Of course, they obeyed Indra.

'You are right. I don't know what I'm doing. I came here only because I didn't know what else to do.' Indra could feel the tears burning their way down his face. 'You are right,' he repeated, coming close to Vayu, 'but it doesn't give you the right to kill me.'

Before anyone realized what was happening, Indra stabbed Vayu with a knife that he had been hiding on his person.

Vayu fell back against the board, shocked. 'You stupid old fool! It was not me.'

'You had motive! No one else wanted to kill me as much as you.'

'You fool!' Vayu cried and lunged towards Indra.

Indra fell, trying to catch his breath. 'I'm going to choke you,' said Vayu, clinging on to his wound, the knife still jammed into his body. 'You are dead.'

Indra staggered and tried to reach for Vayu's hair. The ship continued to roll …

Vayu lost control. Indra took the opportunity and used his foot to make Vayu trip. As Vayu groaned in pain, Indra grabbed him by the throat and tried to choke him.

'You will die, you little shit. You went against me. You tried to kill me.'

'I … didn't … do … it,' said Vayu, gasping.

'Then who was it? Who could it be? Who could it be if not you?'

And then Indra and Vayu both heard it. Loud and clear.

'It was me!'

Indra turned his face up. He let go off Vayu's throat as he looked up and saw the person who had tried to get him killed.

It was Sachi.

CHAPTER TWENTY-EIGHT

The bitter cold was causing Prahlad a lot of agony, but Dhriti was in worse shape. A river flowed like a green and black ribbon in front of the cove where they were resting. They had been travelling for a while now, letting go of luxuries and having only each other for support.

Prahlad had gathered oxen fur for Dhriti and himself. It had been days since they had gone into hiding, staying away from people who might ask why an Asura was wandering. Until now, no one seemed to be chasing them. Yet, Prahlad woke up screaming in fear every day.

Whenever Prahlad heard villagers talking about a wanted boy travelling with a girl, he ran from there. He knew the ravens had spread the word.

'I'm cold,' Dhriti said, shivering despite the fur covering her.

'Don't worry. We are about to reach.'

'What makes you think he will allow us to enter?'

'He is Shiva. He lets everyone enter.'

Dhriti narrowed her eyes and stared at him, exhausted. 'We could have gone to Pataal.'

'Believe me, that's no place to live. We will make a home here. We will have kids here. We will get married here.'

'If it's in that order, I'll be witch-hunted.'

Both of them laughed.

Dhriti's hand, cold as it was, touched Prahlad's face. She smiled. 'I hope you know what you are doing.'

To be honest, Prahlad felt lost. He felt abandoned. He had always been protected and offered comfort. And now he was in the most neglected part of Illavarti.

Perhaps that's the point of growing up.

Prahlad could see that Dhriti had fallen asleep again. He went back to warming up some eels and cooking the fish he had just caught. He waited for the sun to come up.

They would leave the next day.

Prahlad had been carrying Dhriti on his shoulders because she no longer had the strength to walk. Her feet were frozen and she craved warmth. Prahlad knew they had to get to Shiva's fort soon.

So, mustering up spirit and courage, Prahlad kept walking, carrying Dhriti. His eyes fought to stay open, his body demanded rest. Out in the cold, the wolves howled and the vultures waited for them to fall so that they could rip their bodies open.

Just when Prahlad was about to give up, he saw the large fort with a trishul emblazoned on the flag. He smiled and managed to walk to the fort, crying at the sight of the black castle made of iron. Located on the edge of a cliff, it had several settlements around it.

'Save us! Save us!' he yelled before collapsing. Dhriti was by his side.

Prahlad woke up to the warmth of a fire. He looked around frantically to see that he was in a cabin made of wood, with a fire burning on the side. There was some broth kept near him, which he ate with gusto. He noticed that Dhriti was not there.

Instead, there was a young man with a trishul symbol on his chest staring back at him. He had a patch of hair in the middle of his head, which was tied up, while the sides had been shaved.

'Ah, they were right,' he said, looking straight into Prahlad's eyes. 'You are an Asura.'

'Where's ... where's ...'

'She's resting in the women's cabin. Did you not think of using a sledge, especially if you had to travel a great distance? Or maybe considered getting a yak to make the travel easier?'

'This is the first time I have come north. And probably the last.'

The man chuckled. 'What is an Asura doing here?'

'I seek Lord Shiva.'

'And here I am!'

Prahlad was shocked. 'I can't believe it.'

'Well, you are not the first one.' After a pause, he asked, 'Tell me why you are here before I treat you like a prisoner.

The entire camp is, well ... not very happy to hear mention of Asuras.'

'I understand. We have not left a good impression,' Prahlad said. 'Well, I am Prahlad, the son of Hiranyakashyap.'

Shiva narrowed his eyes. 'The son who killed his father?'

'Yes.'

'You are on our side, I believe.'

'I'm on the side of Dharma.' Prahlad showed Shiva his Shrivatsa ring. 'I believe in Lord Vishnu, and I need your help to restore Dharma. I can't stay for very long, but let me tell you the story from the beginning.'

And Prahlad spoke about everything—about Narasimha's crowning, about the love of his life being killed, about Vaashkal. By the end, he was almost out of breath. Shiva hadn't spoken a single word, but he had been listening intently, especially to the accounts of the horrific crimes that Narasimha had committed for the sake of power.

'That's quite heavy,' Shiva said. 'Quite heavy.'

'Yes. That's why I have come to you for assistance.'

Shiva looked at him with soft eyes. 'The thing is, boy, you might say anything, but I do not know how true it is. It could be a fairy tale for all I know. You have come here asking about a sword that my predecessor ensured was kept hidden and out of sight. If anyone is going to make a decision about killing Narasimha, it will be me. I will help you, but I need some confirmation. I am sending a raven to an outpost close to Kashyapuri. If the raven verifies what you have told me, then I believe we will need to act. Don't worry, you don't have to do it alone. Lord Rudra has clearly stated in his journal that the Avatar of this age must be killed. Thus, it is our duty.'

After hearing Shiva, Prahlad was glad he had come there and decided to be honest with him.

'Where did you hear about the sword though?' Shiva asked.

'People talk. Many of them know, and many dismiss it as a myth.'

'Well, I'm glad you didn't dismiss it. What people call a myth is usually poorly documented history. We have withheld information about the sword because we don't want everyone hunting for it. Imagine the power of a sword that can kill an Avatar. It can bring down any king, kingdom, empire and sorcerer. That's the kind of power it wields.'

Prahlad understood what Shiva was saying. He smiled. 'Thank you. With your help, we can definitely achieve what we want to.'

'Yes.'

With that, Shiva left. Prahlad lay down again, closing his eyes and sleeping peacefully after a long time.

CHAPTER TWENTY-NINE

Narasimha was feeling miserable. He had no idea where he was, whether it was a prison or some other place. He had been thrown there and pushed and shoved around. He wanted to take a deep breath, he wanted to move, but he couldn't. All he could do was blink, with his arms and legs remaining stationary.

He had no idea how long it had been, whether it had been days or weeks. The guards would come to give him water and food and then leave.

I have to do something.

Though he wanted to take action, his body wouldn't cooperate. One day, he had lifted a finger and felt better. The next day, he had lifted another finger and felt as if there was hope for him. But that had been the extent of his progress.

Today, however, was different. He had been able to move his hand. A smile formed on his lips as he felt energy zapping through his open hand. He looked outside the large window, past the grills.

I can do it. I can summon the power of thunder.

Thunder roared as Narasimha stared at the sky.

Come on.

He tried to clench the thunder. The clouds gave way and rain started pelting the ground.

The guards outside became alert. 'What is going on?' one of them asked.

Another guard answered: 'Lord Vaashkal said that if something like this happens, we must call him and ensure he is here.'

'Don't worry, I don't think he can do much except summon a storm.'

But Nara didn't give up. He tried to move his hand more, to destroy the walls with thunder. His memory had begun to return and he knew if he could do it, he'd be able to drop down into the sewers and exit the city from there, just lying in the waste. He knew it would be tough.

And then, just like that, he gave up. As he closed his eyes, tears fell to the floor. Nara was so defeated that he was unable to wipe his face.

'I heard you summoned thunder.'

Nara woke up to a familiar voice. He had to look around to see who had spoken. In the shadows, on a stool, was Andhaka. His skull was present, and his eyes were black, just watching him.

'That's quite commendable,' Andhaka sighed. 'You have tried to kill me a hundred times, and each time you have failed. That's quite sad.' After a pause, he continued. 'Hmm, there's one problem I see in Vaashkal's plan. If only he had given me the power to control thunder, it would have been fine. But you still have it. I think I understand why he did that.'

Why? Nara wanted to ask. Anger was bubbling inside him. He wanted to kill Andhaka, who he knew was a coward. Nara berated himself for not having been able to see through the betrayal earlier. He realized that his greed for power had made him blind to everything else.

'Ever since you have been locked up here, we have been convincing the cabinet and the people to accept me as the king.' Andhaka sighed. 'And it has worked. The votes are in my favour. The fact that I am Hiranyakashyap's son definitely helped. Also, since I am his older child, I have the first right to the throne. The usurper was always a distraction, a temporary measure, as Vaashkal puts it. Hmm.'

You are going to die. I will kill you and your friend.

'I'll be crowned the king and it'll be over,' Andhaka said. 'I will undertake a hero's campaign. After all, I am Skanda, the hero this country deserves, the mythical giant of heroic proportions. I will take control of the entire country if I have to. There's already too many Devas and Asuras, if you ask me. Only good people should reign, you know.'

If you think you are among the good people, you are wrong. You are the worst.

'I will make the country proud. I wonder what it will be like to rule the world. Imagine, a blind man who got rid of his handicap, conquered his fears and a king who ran away from his duties because he was tired. That's the story we are concocting,' Andhaka said. 'Hmm, I think you should rest now. And try to have a good time here because you are going to stay for a while.'

And then Andhaka brought out Nara's mane. As he knelt down and made Nara wear it, he said, 'I do not want you to forget that this is how the Avatar of Vishnu was destroyed.'

Andhaka laughed and then disappeared out of the prison lock.

Nara clenched his hand as tightly as he could. He remembered that not long ago he had thought of himself as a hero doing the right thing. Perhaps no one who had power was capable of doing the right thing. Perhaps he had been doing the wrong thing all along, which was why Prahlad was against him.

Prahlad ...

Nara knew Prahlad was being hunted on his orders. He could be killed. Nara regretted issuing those orders, but he hadn't thought twice about it when he had been in power.

Nara sighed. His eyes closed and he fell asleep.

Nara woke up to thunder raging in the sky. He smiled. He hadn't summoned it, but he could do so now.

Waking up from his sleep, he tried to stretch his hand out. He had studied medicine and knew what aconite did to the body. He remembered treating a person in the north a long time ago.

He needed adrenaline to reduce the effects of aconite. And he could have adrenaline coursing through his veins by shocking himself. The idea scared him, but he knew he had to do it.

His hand was definitely better now. He could also move his body a little. After a bit of a struggle, he raised his arm to the window, towards the thunder.

I summon thee. Come on!

In an instant, a flash of light struck the windows and broke through the walls of the prison, leaving behind a trail of carcasses and broken stones and pebbles. Outside, the guards began to open the doors. Nara could see the sewer water that headed straight out of the kingdom.

The guards entered Nara's prison room. Nara clenched his fist. Thunder zapped through the sky and struck them one by one, killing them.

He clenched his fist again and closed his eyes, allowing the thunder to take control of him. He felt his power and energy coming back.

When the thunder stopped, Nara was on his feet, overlooking the broken and disparaged prison wall. He still felt weak, but he was able to limp forward. A smile appeared on his face as he felt ready to take over the world once again …

But the next instant he felt weak again and fell …

Into the sewer water.

Nara was covered in filth. He could feel himself being carried through the water. Managing to drag himself out of it, he saw that the skyline of Kashyapuri had receded into the background. Not long ago, he had entered the city through this very channel to kill Hiranyakashyap, and now he was escaping using the same route.

I need my energy back.

A storm was brewing. As Nara struggled to get up, and failed each time, he could sense a pair of eyes following him. Was it a fox or a squirrel? He couldn't be sure. He looked up to see what it was.

It was a woman he knew very well.

'Nara,' Parvati gasped, 'what in God's name happened to you?'

CHAPTER THIRTY

Prahlad was jerked out of sleep by a loud noise.

He could hear cries and strange crackling sounds. He rushed outside to see what was happening and couldn't believe his eyes. Large rocks, set on fire, were rolling about. Many huts and the castle walls had been damaged. Soldiers who looked like mercenaries were attacking and stabbing people.

The soldiers of Shiva were fighting.

What is going on?

The bell was ringing, not that the mayhem and bloodshed needed to be announced.

Dhriti.

He rushed towards the quarters, where Dhriti was, and opened the door. One of the attackers had already entered. Dhriti had stabbed him in the neck with a knitting needle, sending out a spray of blood.

'I believe we have been attacked.'

'You don't say, my love?'

A soldier appeared behind him just then, but Dhriti rushed and stabbed him with the same needle. He fell back. Prahlad grabbed hold of the dead man's sword and handed the dagger to Dhriti.

'We need to leave,' she said. It sounded like a command.

'But the sword? We need to find Shiva.'

It was not hard to find him. Shiva was fighting three attackers with his trishul.

Who is responsible for this?

A volley of arrows rained down from the sky. Prahlad pushed Dhriti in the corner to be saved. He helped the women and children find refuge before trying to head towards Shiva. Just then, the gates opened and he saw someone familiar.

It was none other than Shantaram, a walking stick in his hand and an array of soldiers on their stallions ridging ahead of him, ready to attack.

Prahlad should have guessed. The giant had cast him aside but not killed him. He must have lost a leg in the process, but that hadn't stopped him from chasing Prahlad. And since he had the king's scroll, he was able to muster local mercenaries to fight Shiva and his soldiers at his fort.

Prahlad was sure that Vaashkal and Narasimha had breached a boundary by attacking Shiva's fort, a sacred place. But they hadn't cared because all they wanted was *him*.

'We need to run before they get to us.'

Prahlad locked the cabin where the women and children were and navigated through an array of fighters to get to Shiva. Dhriti was behind him, the dagger clutched close to her heart.

By now, Shiva had been stabbed multiple times in the chest. He was on the ground. Prahlad yelled before jumping on the attackers and stabbing them, while Dhriti punched and kicked. She grabbed a crossbow and shot the mercenaries who came too close.

Prahlad held Shiva. 'My lord, you are …'

Shiva coughed blood. 'I don't … Parvati … save the fort.'

I can't. Shantaram has got too many of them.

'It is Narasimha. He did it. Tell me where the sword is. I will ensure he is killed with it.'

Shiva pulled Prahlad closer and whispered the location into his ears before his eyes closed and he lay lifeless.

'Let's go,' Prahlad said to Dhriti. 'We need to make a run for it.'

Immediately outside the fort, a lane zigzagged down to a cold lake in which a willow grew. This point also doubled up as the docks, beyond which boats used for fishing were lined up.

Leaving behind all the smoke and fury, Prahlad and Dhriti sprinted to the willow.

'Where are we going? The horses are on the other end,' Dhriti said.

'The sword,' Prahlad responded. 'Get a boat ready. I'll get the sword and end this misery that has been following us for a while now.'

Dhriti nodded grudgingly and made her way into the stream to get to the boats. Prahlad looked at a spot next to the willow. It was the opening to the cave where the sword lay, easy to miss unless one looked closely.

Prahlad walked into the cave and reached a large bridge made of ice-glass. It had no ledges. One wrong step would send him to his death in the dark depths below. The rocks around seemed unsteady.

Prahlad trudged forward carefully, trying to catch a glimpse of the coveted sword. It was no myth. It was as beautiful as he had expected it to be. Made of bones and iron, the sword stood there guarded by the rocks. A stream of light coming in from a spot directly above it illuminated it.

You are mine now.

Prahlad got closer and managed to get his hands on the sword. But, as soon as he turned, he saw someone standing on the other side of the bridge. Someone he hadn't expected.

Shantaram.

The sword, Prahlad felt, was heavy and light at the same time, glistening with a beauty that seemed unreal. It felt like it was an extension of Prahlad.

'You are going to die,' Shantaram said. 'I'll ensure it, and I'll get that sword to Lord Vaashkal as a souvenir.'

Prahlad confidently stepped on to the bridge. 'Fight me then.'

'Oh, sure. You aren't worried?'

'I'm done worrying.'

Shantaram limped forward and parried with Prahlad. Regardless of his handicap, he was very tough and the better swordsman. The sound of their swords clashing echoed in the cave.

Prahlad decided to swing his sword and hit Shantaram's damaged leg.

Shantaram laughed. 'Hah! I don't have it.'

Both Prahlad and Shantaram had maintained their balance well. They knew that one wrong step would mean death. That's when Prahlad had an idea.

As Shantaram came forward to attack, Prahlad deflected his sword and shoved him off the bridge. Shantaram's shrieks drowned in a second as he fell into oblivion.

The bridge, unable to handle so much pressure, started giving way. Prahlad leapt towards the ledge and managed to haul himself up to safety. Breathing deeply, he felt peace he had not experienced in a long time.

He exited the cave to see a shining sun. Dhriti was ready with the boat. She began rowing away from land once Prahlad sat down. There were arrows being shot towards them, but they missed and were lost in the water.

Prahlad looked at the fort, which had gone up in smoke. He felt bad for Shiva. Holding the sword close, he was just happy that he had been able to retrieve it.

It's time to meet Narasimha.

CHAPTER THIRTY-ONE

Indra was sitting alone in the captain's lodge as the ship rolled.

He didn't know whether to cry or feel anger. His wife had tried to kill him, but he didn't want to hurt her back. He didn't feel the rage he had expected. All he wanted to do was contemplate.

What was he doing so wrong? Perhaps he was not a good person. Perhaps he had made too many mistakes.

Indra sat glued to his chair when there was a knock on the door. He didn't answer, but the door opened. His eyes were drawn to the face that appeared … it was his wife. She looked concerned.

Though he could have, Indra didn't have Sachi locked up. The guards had held up their weapons when she had accepted responsibility. Indra, who had had to apologize to Vayu as well, had asked everyone to leave her.

'I think it's safe to say that I'm sorry,' Sachi said.

'What if I had died?'

'You are Indra. You wouldn't have died. You have faced more assassination attempts than anyone else.'

'And you took that chance?'

'I wanted you to realize that people around you are not happy.'

'That's not the way to do it.'

'Really? You have been going around asking people about the mistakes you have made. The old Indra would have rebuked me and retaliated. This time, he didn't. The old Indra would have escaped, but this time he didn't. You have grown as a person. Look, even your hair is white now.'

Indra chuckled. He knew she was right. Revenge was not important to him anymore. All he wanted to know was why she had done this. He felt empathy instead of rage.

Have I really changed?

'So, it was just to make me realize what I was doing wrong?' he asked.

'You asked us to accompany you into an ocean, you left your kingdom behind. Earlier, you would run away alone. This time you made the people close to you escape as well. Is that what a king does?' She paused. 'I was angry, too, I'll be honest. Jayanti's death was your fault, and you refused to accept it.'

Indra nodded. 'You are right. It was my fault. I should have talked to Nara, tried to hear him out. Suffice to say, it's too late now. The man is after my throat.'

'Then you fight him back, but you don't retaliate. We are too old for this. When I ordered the assassination, I was double-minded. I knew it was wrong, but I wanted to teach you a lesson. In the process, I became you. I became Indra, when I should have just been myself.'

Indra had never thought about the agony he was inflicting on those around him. He nodded and got up to embrace his wife. 'I'm sorry. I shouldn't have left you that day when I killed Vritra. I shouldn't have retaliated against Nara. I shouldn't have tried to get away. I am a failure.'

Sachi pulled back. 'No man is a failure if he admits that he has failed. Only arrogance brings good men down on their knees.'

He smiled. 'I don't think there was ever a serpent.'

'Perhaps there is.'

'Perhaps it doesn't matter,' he said. 'What matters is that I should be with my people.'

With a sigh, he added, 'I almost killed my brother, gods. It isn't the first time though. We always get into a scuffle once in a blue moon.'

Sachi smiled. 'So, where to?'

Indra arched his eyebrows. 'Home, my love. Let us go home.'

CHAPTER THIRTY-TWO

Parvati and the rest of the Matrikas were camping on the outskirts of Kashyapuri. They had kept a bonfire going and the forest fulfilled all their requirements as they plotted their attack on the city. They knew they had to be swift and discreet, they couldn't just go on a rampage and attack anyone and everyone. They also had to account for the several soldiers positioned inside.

And now they had Narasimha.

Parvati had no idea how he had managed to escape through the sewer channel. He told her his story whenever he had enough energy. By now, Parvati knew how he had become the king and how he was betrayed by Andhaka. The way Nara described Andhaka made it clear to the Matrikas that they had to be careful in dealing with him.

'How is Prahlad? What is he up to?' Chamundi asked.

'I sent a party out to kill him.' Nara sounded drained. He had been unwell, unable to move much, even though he was fed well and given the right medicines. 'He tried to dethrone me.'

'Is he dead?' Brahmani asked quietly. 'It's surprising because you two seemed to be close.'

'We are. We were, I mean.' Nara shook his head. 'But … he's totally against me and I have to save myself. I should not have done it.'

The Matrikas nodded in unison. They did not tell Nara that Prahlad could be Skanda—the child who could save the country of Illavarti.

After they left Nara's tent to allow him to rest, Brahmani asked: 'We need to start asking him the right questions about the kingdom. We need to get in and do what we came here for.'

'Let him rest,' Parvati said.

Brahmani narrowed her gaze. 'You are quiet. What happened?'

'Nothing.'

'You are stalling. Why?'

Parvati clenched her jaw. 'Um, the fact that we are this close makes me want to not kill Andhaka. He's still my son. He's still my boy. And I just … I don't know. I am getting cold feet.'

Brahmani put her hand on Parvati's shoulders. 'It's all right. We get it. We also went through the same thing, but we realized that it's best to do what we set out to do.'

'Yes,' Parvati nodded.

Also, we need to save Prahlad from Narasimha. We can't let the boy be a victim.'

'Of course. But let's not tell Nara anything.'

In the days to come, Nara told the Matrikas more about the empire: the points from where they could infiltrate, where the gateways were, what shifts the soldiers kept. The Matrikas now had a fair idea about where Andhaka lived and how to get there.

Narasimha told them everything in the hope of being crowned king again. He didn't want to be branded a deserter. There were many people who respected him and cared for him. He couldn't just leave.

Finally, one night Parvati decided it was time. She explained the plan to the Matrikas. 'You will jump from here,' she said, pointing at a map, 'and I will attack the watchtower. We have to enter through the sewers, come to the back door and enter quietly. We then have to take the guards down and move to the third floor.'

They all listened intently, while Nara stood weakly leaning on his cane for support.

'Nara, I believe you won't be joining us.'

'I want to. I want to kill Vaashkal with my own hands for betraying me.' He paused, unable to stand steady. 'But I think I should stay back. I'm still recovering.'

In the dead of the night, they continued to discuss the plot, eliminating all loopholes. And finally, they had a foolproof plan.

On the appointed day, when they were preparing to depart for Kashyapuri, an arrow came flying into the tent and stabbed one of the Matrikas in the chest.

Brahmani cried out in pain and collapsed. Parvati rushed outside her tent with Narasimha and Chamundi by her side.

In front of them, mounted on a horse and accompanied by Vaashkal and several soldiers, was Andhaka. He looked tougher than ever and his skin was translucent. Next to him was an orange-haired boy who was smiling widely.

Nara limped forward, his teeth bared and his mane glistening. 'You found us.'

'And we found you!' Vaashkal clapped his hands in joy. 'I never expected to find you so easily, that too here, being tended to by a bunch of women.'

'We came here to find you, but we found more. Hmm,' Andhaka grimaced. 'I suppose you refuse to just let it go and die quietly. You need to learn when to give up.'

He dismounted from his horse. His soldiers were ready to fight with crossbows, shields and blades. It was almost fifty of them against a handful of Matrikas and a weak Narasimha. The odds were skewed in Andhaka's favour.

'I am going to end you all,' Andhaka declared.

'And I will leave you to it. I have better things to do than to fight. My men will take care of you.' Vaashkal said with a wicked grin.

Parvati smiled. *Let's begin.*

Arrows began to fly from left to right. Nara threw away his cane and brought down the thunder and storms, hitting many of the soldiers with it, to support the Matrikas as they battled with Andhaka.

Nara saw a couple of soldiers heading towards the Matrikas. He roared and attacked them. One of the soldiers tried to stab him, but Nara managed to deflect the soldier and sent thunder cracking though him.

I need to chase Vaashkal. He needs to die.

Narasimha channelled electricity through his fingers to shock the soldiers, stopping only when he thought that the Matrikas would be able to handle the rest. He rushed towards Vaashkal on one of the horse neighing nearby.

As he closed in on Vaashkal, he realized that the slimy man was armed with poisoned arrows. Nara could see the green tinge of evil smoke swirling out of them. Vaashkal turned and shot at Nara, missing narrowly, but then he let loose another arrow that hit Nara on the shoulder.

Nara fell off the horse. He groaned as he pulled out the poisoned arrow. Aware that he didn't have a lot of time before the paralysis took over his body again, he summoned thunder and crafted a lightning bolt out of it. He aimed it at Vaashkal.

The lightning bolt struck Vaashkal and electrocuted him instantly. He fell to the ground.

Nara rushed to see if Vaashkal was dead or not. He noticed that Vaashkal was barely moving. He knelt next to the man, whose skin had been burnt because of the strong jolt of electricity. His eyes, however, were still moving. He was breathing his last.

'You know that when you get electrocuted like that, your blood literally boils. That's the pain you are feeling right now. I hope you die,' Nara said and left without turning back even once.

Strangely, he felt both triumph and trepidation.

Parvati was using all her moves and energy with her spear, but Andhaka's fists and shield were proving to be tough. He grabbed Brahmani by the throat and threw her away like a piece of meat, and then he threw Parvati's shield away too before pushing her out of the way.

'You are going to face my wrath,' he said, grabbing Chamundi and hitting her with his shield. As she fell, he brought the shield down on her throat and pushed, trying to choke her.

Brahmani stood up and looked at Parvati. 'I'm going to distract him. You attack.'

Parvati nodded. Brahmani hurled herself at Andhaka, lashing out at his eyes and making him writhe in pain. Parvati skid between Andhaka's legs and brought her spear down on his feet, slashing his and leaving deep gashes.

Andhaka growled and threw Brahmani down on Parvati. Both the Matrikas groaned.

'He has become too powerful,' Parvati noted.

By the time they stood up, Narasimhi and Chamundi were fighting him. Andhaka used his shield to hit them and break their bones. And then he twisted Narasimhi's neck.

Brahmani yelled in horror. So did Parvati.

'We need to surprise him to bring him down.'

He was about to hurt Chamundi, too, when Parvati yelled: 'Give me a platform to jump.'

Brahmani and Parvati both ran towards Andhaka. Brahmani, a few steps ahead, suddenly knelt before Andhaka, who was surprised because he had noticed that she wasn't armed. Parvati used Brahmani's shoulder as a platform to jump with her spear held high ...

Andhaka tried to pull his shield up, but Chamundi didn't let him raise it.

Parvati stabbed him right in the eye and pushed the spear deep into his skull, killing him.

Andhaka was lost for a second, and then he fell.

Parvati looked at him, thinking about how she had had cold feet a short while ago. But seeing Andhaka like that, she was sure that she had done the right thing. There was no shame in admitting it.

Narasimhi, unfortunately, was dead.

But the fight was over. It was done.

CHAPTER THIRTY-THREE

A few months later ...

Prahlad was back in the north. This time, he was nowhere close to Shiva's fort. Travelling alone, he was in the Mahendragiri mountains, trying to find the perfect hiding spot for the sword.

Prahlad was sure he wanted to hide the sword, even though he knew it would ensure his victory in every war and every fight. And he was sure that it was not meant to fall into a layperson's hands.

He had come to this decision after the incident with Narasimha. He was sure that the sword had served its purpose for the time being.

Narasimha was sleeping peacefully. It had been weeks since Andhaka and Vaashkal had accosted the Matrikas and him.

Meanwhile, things weren't stable in the kingdom. Nara was doing his best to ensure that trade and economy recovered and that he had a reliable council of ministers to help him. He knew the city needed strong administration and that he had to forget about the seizure of Amravati. But Nara's days were not over. He was ready to take the throne back, ready to defend himself if needed.

His body, however, still hadn't recovered. Despite the comfort of the rugs and blankets, he felt weak. He would often limp and his arms would tremble. He was not himself. The good part was that his nightmares had stopped. His medicines were strong enough to lull him into a deep sleep.

Nara was glad.

However, tonight was different. He didn't have to slip into a dream to feel terror. He was standing face-to-face with it, opposite an armed intruder whose face, except the eyes, was concealed.

'Who are you?' Nara asked. There was pin-drop silence, except the chirp of the crickets.

The intruder pulled off his mask.

'Prahlad' Nara swallowed a lump. 'It's good to see you, boy. It's been a while.'

Nara looked at the sword in Prahlad's hand; he had never seen anything like that. Taken aback by its quality, he said, 'I believe you are here to kill me.'

'I'm still conflicted,' Prahlad said. He looked stern and scarred.

'But you can't kill me. I cannot be killed,' Nara said, displaying the Shrivatsa symbol on his chest.

'I don't think that's true. I have a solution for that.'

Nara, surprised at the conviction with which Prahlad spoke, felt scared. 'How did you manage to enter?'

'You told the Matrikas everything about the city and about its security arrangements. I knew when to enter discreetly.'

'You are doing the wrong thing. You have been opposing me even while we have been killing enemies. I am a better man now,' Nara pleaded. 'I don't think this is necessary. We can talk about it. Please, let's just sit …'

'So that you can kill me? No.'

'You tried to usurp me. I was threatened, Prahlad. What did you expect?'

'I expected you to do the right thing. I was always looking for Lord Vishnu's path of justice in your actions, and then I realized that I needed to be that justice. The people deserve that.' He sighed and continued. 'After you killed Indra's daughter, I knew you had let power go to your head.'

'I'm the same,' Nara said with a smile. The sword was inches away from his neck. 'Don't you realize? We are bound to each other, you and me.'

Prahlad arched his eyebrows. 'Have you really changed?'

'You will see the difference tomorrow. I will show you the changes I plan to implement, all of which are non-violent and adhere to Dharma. Please, understand that you are doing the wrong thing.'

Prahlad's eyes softened. 'You are right. I … erm …' he sighed as he began to pull the sword away from Nara's neck. But then he noticed Nara's hand and froze.

'What happened?' Nara asked, trying to study Prahlad's expression.

'You are not wearing your ring.'

'What?'

'Your ring,' Prahlad said, showing Nara the one on his own finger, which Nara had gifted him. 'The ring of Dharma, the ring—'

'I must have lost it. It's been quite a hectic—'

His sentence was cut short by Prahlad, who sliced his throat. Blood spurted out as Nara struggled.

He spluttered and gasped until his eyes closed and his grip around the bedsheets loosened. His last words were: 'I can see her.'

Prahlad broke down and sent up a silent prayer for Nara.

I hope you find peace, my friend. I really hope you do.

A few days after Nara's death, as the sun set, Indra waited outside Amravati with his army. With his allies and Vayu by his side, Indra was ready to strike... There were thousands of soldiers behind him.

'So, when do we plan to ride in and challenge Narasimha to a battle?'

'When the scouts inform us. He's supposed to attack anytime now. And it's almost weird that he has not,' Indra said.

They saw a mare riding towards them. It was a messenger, but not Indra's scout. And it was a young girl! She dismounted and handed a scroll to one of Indra's soldiers, who blocked her approach.

'What is the meaning of this?' Indra asked.

'A letter from the king. About a truce and his not wanting to battle.'

'Narasimha has forfeited?' Indra was confused.

'Not Narasimha. Prahlad. He's the new king of Kashyapuri. Of the realm, in fact.'

'Child,' Indra asked, 'what happened to Narasimha?'

She smiled and then said, 'He's dead. King Prahlad clearly said that he wants no violence. He wants everyone to live in harmony and peace. He, in fact, wants to talk to you about how to strengthen trade relations and open the market to foreigners so more revenue comes in. He wants to rule on the side.'

'Dear, dear …' Indra nodded. 'Erm, sure.'

'But in return, he has clearly stated that he wants no betrayal and no backstabbing. According to him, this country deserves better than scheming politicians and naysayers. This country doesn't deserve just one hero, it deserves heroes. He wants you to be one as well.' With that, the girl jumped back on to her horse.

Indra was befuddled.

'I believe we should attack,' Vayu said. 'We should take advantage of this weak leadership and grab what's ours.'

Indra blinked. 'Or perhaps we share what is ours. Isn't that a better thing?' he said to Vayu, who nodded.

'And I thought I would push you to your death in this war as revenge for what you did to me earlier,' Vayu said with a smile.

Indra chuckled. 'Let's go home, brother. It's time to rest.'

'Finally!'

'Yes. Finally.'

Prahlad reached the summit and entered the cold cave-like structure that had no ceiling. There were glaciers all around. Though it was freezing, Prahlad was warm under the fur he was wearing.

He began to recollect how he had taken the kingdom. It had taken time. How Parvati had stayed at the Shiva's fort, taking control of the place and beginning to build it up again.

Prahlad's mind raced through recent events, even his proposal to Dhriti. He had finally had the courage to ask her, knowing that she would not refuse him.

He kept the sword on the slab, stepped back and looked at it. It still glistened with Narasimha's blood. It still held the memory of violence.

He began to descend, headed back to his home, his kingdom and his fiancée …

He knew that one day, years later, the sword would be used again. That time, he hoped, it would serve a better purpose.

Not to kill an Avatar, but to help one.

ACKNOWLEDGEMENTS

I would like to thank my readers.

I would also like to thank my parents, who encouraged my writing and pushed me to become the writer I am today. I am also thankful to the Redink Literary Agency for helping this series find a home at HarperCollins India. This is the last book of the series with them, and HarpeerCollins has ensured the series' popularity among readers. I am grateful to my team, Hubhawks, who helped create a wonderful cover. I am also grateful to my Chenchita, Kiran Malik, for being a pillar during my writing process and helping me work through my thoughts. She's been nothing but a miracle for the writer in me.

All in all, I would like to thank everyone who has supported the Narasimha Trilogy in any form and way. It means a lot. Hope you enjoyed the last of the series.

ABOUT THE AUTHOR

Kevin Missal wrote his first book at the age of fourteen, and at twenty-two, the St. Stephen's graduate was a bestselling author with the first two books in his Kalki series, which were runaway successes. Kevin loves fantasy fiction and has always been a fan of mythology. His books have been featured in publications like *The Sunday Guardian, The New Indian Express* and *Millennium Post*. He lives in Gurugram and he can be contacted at kevin.s.missal@gmail.com.

30 Years *of*

 HarperCollins *Publishers* India

At HarperCollins, we believe in telling the best stories and finding the widest possible readership for our books in every format possible. We started publishing 30 years ago; a great deal has changed since then, but what has remained constant is the passion with which our authors write their books, the love with which readers receive them, and the sheer joy and excitement that we as publishers feel in being a part of the publishing process.

Over the years, we've had the pleasure of publishing some of the finest writing from the subcontinent and around the world, and some of the biggest bestsellers in India's publishing history. Our books and authors have won a phenomenal range of awards, and we ourselves have been named Publisher of the Year the greatest number of times. But nothing has meant more to us than the fact that millions of people have read the books we published, and somewhere, a book of ours might have made a difference.

As we step into our fourth decade, we go back to that one word – a word which has been a driving force for us all these years.

Read.

Harper
Collins

HARPER
PERENNIAL

HARPER
BUSINESS

HARPER
BLACK

हार्पर
हिन्दी

HarperCollins
Children'sBooks

HARPER
DESIGN

HARPER
VANTAGE

Harper
Sport